Then Fred says, "Yeah, you look great this year, Lacey *Underwire*. You're the eighth wonder of the world." He makes a big show of staring at my chest, like he's trying to puzzle out a math problem. "Or should I make that eighth and ninth wonders of the world?"

"You're hysterical, Fred," I say, "like no one's ever made that joke before. It's Under*hill*, not Underwire."

"But it should be." I hear him laugh as I finally take a seat all the way at the back, the bus driver having yelled at me to "Just sit down!" like, eight times already. "It should be Lacey Underwire."

And so it starts.

me, in between

by Lauren Baratz-Logsted

ALADDIN MIX
NEW YORK   LONDON   TORONTO   SYDNEY

This book is a work of fiction. Any references to historical events, real people, or real locales are used fictitiously. Other names, characters, places, and incidents are the product of the author's imagination, and any resemblance to actual events or locales or persons, living or dead, is entirely coincidental.

ALADDIN MIX
Simon & Schuster Children's Publishing Division
1230 Avenue of the Americas, New York, NY 10020
Copyright © 2008 by Lauren Baratz-Logsted
All rights reserved, including the right of reproduction
in whole or in part in any form.
ALADDIN PAPERBACKS and related logo are registered
trademarks of Simon & Schuster, Inc.
ALADDIN MIX is a trademark of Simon & Schuster, Inc.
Designed by Jessica Sonkin
The text of this book was set in Lomba Book.
Manufactured in the United States of America
First Aladdin Mix edition March 2008
2 4 6 8 10 9 7 5 3 1
Library of Congress Control Number 2007931047
ISBN-13: 978-1-4169-5068-4
ISBN-10: 1-4169-5068-0

For Sue Estabrook and Kaethe Douglas,
the two best readers a
writer could dream to have:
with gratitude, friendship, and love

Acknowledgments

Thank you to Pamela Harty for putting up with me—I do know how much I ask. Thank you to Liesa Abrams for helping me make this book the best I could make it—any remaining errors are mine. And to the whole Simon & Schuster team.

Thank you to my mother, Lucille Baratz, for having me; my husband, Greg Logsted, for marrying me; and my daughter, Jackie, for lighting up my world.

1.

TORPEDOES.

Bazooms.

Balloons.

Knockers.

Boobs.

These are just a sampling of the many words that have been used in the last two years by others referring to my breasts . . . my size 36C breasts.

Whenever I try to discuss this with my Dutch grandmother, with whom I've been living since my parents both died in a car crash when I was small, she refers to my chest as *luxe problemen*. English translation: "luxury problems."

I was so young when my parents died that I don't really remember them. They're just pictures in photo albums to me, stories other relatives tell. But I always imagine that if they were alive, they'd *get* things my grandmother simply doesn't.

My grandmother is sixty-eight, swears her champagne blond mushroom-cap hair is its natural color, has blue eyes that see twenty-twenty (just like me), has been known to coach the neighborhood boys at sports, wears housedresses with confidence as though they'll be featured in all the fashion magazines next month, and never lost her accent. She has so much energy, the only time I think of her as being fifty-six years older than me is when she takes her heart medication . . . or when she makes me crazy by not getting something so obvious as my problems with my breasts.

The first time she said this to me, about *luxe problemen*, I asked her what she meant.

She replied, "It's like the millionaire complaining about gas prices for his Rolls-Royce."

"Are you *really* sure it's like that?" I asked.

"Then maybe it's like Midas, complaining that everything he touched turned to gold."

"But that was awful for him!" I said. We'd studied King Midas one year in English class. "Even his food and wine turned to gold when he touched them. The poor man practically starved!"

"Details." She sniffed. "He was probably an alcoholic who ate too much anyway."

"So practically dying of hunger and thirst was an improvement?"

"It's all relative." She shrugged. "Fine. Maybe you're right. Maybe Midas didn't have *luxe problemen* at all. Maybe he just had *problemen*. How about this, then: *Luxe problemen* are like when a girl is beautiful and has the kind of beautiful breasts that any woman would kill for—"

"Yeah, *woman*. How many *girls* do you know who had to get an underwire bra as their first training bra?"

But my grandmother was not to be put off making her case. She went on as though she hadn't heard me. "*Luxe problemen* are like when a girl is beautiful and has the kind of beautiful breasts that any *female* would kill for, and yet all she does is complain about them."

"I'm sorry I said anything," I muttered. "Thanks for your help."

"Anytime."

And I know she meant it when she said it, still means it today. But as much as I know she loves me, as helpful as she is in many ways, I know I won't be trying to talk to my grandmother about my breasts anymore. I'm guessing Nana Anna just doesn't get it.

Like she didn't get it when I was ten and first went through puberty. There I was at age ten—ten! Did you hear me say *ten*??—with big breasts, hairy legs and underarms, and my first period.

My best friend Margot Browning's mom took me to get my first real bra and explained the ins and outs of pads to me, none of which made Margot exactly love me in the moment. Taller than me and two years older, at age fourteen Margot is still flat-chested and periodless. I keep telling her I'd gladly change places with her if I could, but the look on her face always says she can't understand why.

Since Mrs. Browning took care of the breast-containment and bodily-fluid issues, Nana Anna only had one problem to address on her own: the hairiness thing. Honestly. You'd think a woman who dropped hints as to once having led some sort of "resistance movement" as a small child—resisting what, I don't know—and who claimed to be somehow distantly related to Queen Beatrix (of the Netherlands) could deal with a little thing like her granddaughter sprouting hair all over the place.

So how did Nana Anna deal with it?

She hid all the razors and forbade me to go into any drugstores on my own.

"You're not shaving at ten, Lacey!" she announced with a shout.

"Why not?" I shouted back, standing up straight enough to see eye to eye with her. Nana Anna and I are both very short, and she always says that her (lack of) height is one of the reasons she left the Netherlands. "They are giants over there, Lacey," she always tells me. "Next to my countrymen, I am a dwarf."

I try to tell her all the time that the polite term in the United States for that condition is "petite," but there are a lot of Old World words Nana Anna just won't let go of.

"Why not?" I shouted a second time, referring to the hairy legs and pits, and the sudden absence of razors in the house. From where I was sitting, Nana Anna could have used a quick run-over with the razor herself.

"Because you are too young," she said.

"I'm not too young to have a period," I countered. Then I crossed my arms smugly as though about to score a major point. "Technically, I could have a baby now."

"Bite that tongue right out of your mouth or I'll rip it out," she warned. I'd never seen her so mad. Okay, maybe the time I let Margot put my long blond hair into tiny braids before Easter services at church. We unplaited them right before we left for church, and I spent the rest of the day looking like I'd stuck my finger into a socket. Nana Anna wasn't pleased. But somehow this was different.

"I don't want to hear another word about it, Lacey. Ten is just too young. If you start shaving now, you'll be shaving the rest of your life."

"Isn't that the idea?"

"Yes. But it's too soon to start. It will only grow back faster and thicker."

"So? I'll shave every day if I have to."

"Enough. I'll tell you when it's time."

"But doesn't it even matter to you that everyone calls me—"

"What, Lacey? What does everyone call you?"

But I'd stopped myself just in time. There was just no way I was going to tell Nana Anna that my school nickname was Monkey. Knowing Nana Anna, she'd go right down to the school and put some kind of Dutch hex on everybody. Or just yell a lot. It would be so embarrassing. And it wouldn't stop people from saying it. They'd just say it more quietly. And even if they said it so quietly I couldn't hear them? I'd still hear them saying it inside my brain. Having heard it aloud so many times, knowing it's what they all thought, I'd go on hearing it as long as I had hair in places I'd rather not.

So I shut up about needing to shave and bided my time. Then one day—I swear I had nothing to do with it!—Mrs. Browning called the house and told Nana Anna that not letting me shave was like some new kind of child abuse. I don't think Mrs. Browning had any idea what a soft spot she was striking. Nana Anna's greatest fear was that someday, before I was old enough to take care of myself, I'd be taken away from her because some other person would have decided that she was too old, too unfit to care for someone my age. So my grandmother caved. And so it was that on Christmas morning of my tenth year I woke to find my red felt stocking stuffed to the white furry trim with Gillette Venuses and Bics and even an electric razor, just in case I wanted to try to electrocute myself while shaving. (That last bit of sarcasm was, of course, Nana Anna's.) I threw myself at Nana Anna's head and hugged her so hard, she said she wondered why she'd never thought of it sooner, that it was a shame she'd wasted years filling my stockings with chocolate and popcorn balls when a four-pack of disposable razors worked so much better.

I began shaving my legs and armpits for the first time right after Christmas breakfast and, as they say, I never looked back. About to enter eighth grade at Wainscot Academy, the K–12 private school where I've been going since kindergarten, I have the smoothest legs and armpits of the whole student body.

If only I knew what to do about my breasts.

2.

THE HOME WE LIVE IN LOOKS LIKE A
giant gingerbread house, painted pink. This color
scheme was Nana Anna's idea, and she gets her
extension ladder out every spring to do touch-up
work, putting a giant rubber band around the hem
of her skirt to keep the neighbors from seeing up
her housedress. Of course, the rubber band makes it
kind of difficult to climb the ladder.

Inside the house, old and heavy furniture pieces
are crammed into every available space, as though
Nana Anna robbed an antique store. It's not exactly
the furniture I would pick, but I never say this to
Nana Anna, particularly since she gives me free rein
to decorate and redecorate my own room any way I
like. Nana Anna always says, "Your room should be

like a haven, Lacey. So long as you don't put up pictures of naked people or pictures of people doing drugs or pictures of naked people doing drugs, anything goes." This leaves me with a fair amount of leeway, and I take advantage of it. Right now three of my walls are painted dark red—Nana Anna says it will take forever to paint over it, but she let me do it anyway—while the fourth wall is covered with silver contact paper, broken up by eight posters. I have black-and-white sheets on my bed and a red fur throw over the sheets. There's a black and red area rug on the floor, and in the twenty-four small frames of the twin double-hung windows I've pressed stained-glass squares I made for an art class last year, each one depicting a scene from the Harry Potter books. (I got an A for Ambition.) Against one of the red-painted walls is a massive bookcase, holding all my favorite books as well as many I haven't cracked open yet but am dying to. I love to read.

My room is my haven, just as Nana Anna says it should be, and the day I like to leave my haven least is the first day of school.

Most kids I know, sick as it sounds and even though they rarely admit it out loud, look forward to the first day of school. I think they view it as an opportunity to start all over again, a clean slate. But not me. The only way the first day of school is a clean slate for me is in offering a new chance for repeated humiliation.

"Lacey! The bus is here!" Nana Anna yells up the stairs.

"Coming!" I shout, already on the run. I pound down the old wooden staircase, shoving my arms into the sleeves of my navy Wainscot blazer, under which I have on a white blouse and loose navy sweater-vest—loose on purpose. The outfit is completed by the regulation blue, green, black, and white plaid skirt.

"You didn't eat breakfast," Nana Anna objects.

"I'll grab a bagel in the cafeteria," I say, grabbing the brand-new stack of notebooks and binders she holds out as I kiss her on the cheek. I'll worry about cramming them all into my backpack later.

"Why do you have that blazer on?" she asks. "It must be ninety degrees out today." Ah, close-to-autumn in New England. "Surely they won't make you wear the blazer and sweater today. You'll sweat to death."

Can't she see this is my camouflage? Can't she see that the loose sweater-vest and unnecessary blazer are ways to keep people from focusing on my breasts?

"It'll be fine, Nana," I say. "They probably still have the air-conditioning jacked up from the summer."

"But Wainscot doesn't have—"

But I don't let her finish pointing out that Wainscot Academy has no air-conditioning in the classrooms because I'm already racing down the concrete, flower-lined path from our front porch to the curb, climbing the steps onto the bus as the doors close shut behind me.

I'm always late. Margot and I used to do a routine when I got on the bus, scrunching our faces together with our hands while shouting, "Bus driver! Bus driver! My face is caught in the door!" It cracked us up, even if it made some of the other kids look at us like we were geeks. But I don't do that anymore because (1) that's something I did when we were younger, not on the cusp of high school—the last year of middle school totally counts as the cusp, and (2) they redrew the bus routes, and even though Margot's house is just around the corner from ours, her house is no longer on my route.

I start down the aisle, trying to decide where to sit now that Margot is no longer here.

I walk past Patty Fontaine and Deanna Drake, girls in our class who always sneer at me and Margot because they both have perfectly normal-size bodies while Margot and I are, well, extremes.

I walk past all the lower-school kids, who are too young to sit with, and the high school kids, who are just barely too old. Since Wainscot is K–12 but small, all the age groups ride the buses together in one big, happy family. Yeah, right.

I start to walk past two boys in my class who are stretched out so they've each got one whole bench seat to themselves on opposite sides of the aisle from each other: John Fredericks, who I notice has grown kind of cute over the summer, and Fred Johnson, who never knows when to let a bad joke die a natural death.

"You're looking good this year, Lacey," John says with almost a shy smile.

I look at that smile and start thinking that he is not only cute, but also nice, and I think about sitting in the seat next to him. Honestly, why am I always so worried about everything? It's nice having people pay you compliments. What girl wouldn't want that? I'll bet Patty and Deanna would like that, if they were me. But when I turn around, they're too busy smirking and giggling.

Then Fred says, "Yeah, you look great this year, Lacey *Underwire*. You're the eighth wonder of the world." He makes a big show of staring at my chest, like he's trying to puzzle out a math problem. "Or should I make that eighth and ninth wonders of the world?"

"You're hysterical, Fred," I say, "like no one's ever made that joke before. It's Under*hill*, not Underwire."

"But it should be." I hear him laugh as I finally take a seat all the way at the back, the bus driver having yelled at me to "Just sit down!" like, eight times already. "It should be Lacey Underwire."

And so it starts.

3.

WAINSCOT ACADEMY, FOUNDED IN 1908, sits on more than one hundred acres of prime Connecticut real estate. It has more than four hundred students in thirteen grades that move among the eighteen buildings of what was once a boarding school. It has a stone chapel that is thought to be more scenic than religious. It is considered to be elite without being stuffy, and 100 percent of its graduating high school seniors are accepted to four-year colleges and universities. What they do once accepted is entirely up to them.

When I first started at Wainscot in kindergarten, I was five, the typical age for that grade, but first grade revealed me to be such a precocious reader, the faculty and administration finally began to give some thought to Nana Anna's advice to move me ahead a grade. When, by the end of first grade, I was regularly correcting the grammar in the homework printouts the teacher gave us, the school decided to take action, and so the following fall I returned to school as a seven-year-old third grader.

I've been with the kids in my class for five years now, so you'd think they'd get over my being "the girl who skipped a grade," but no such luck. Just because they're all a year older than me—or two years, depending on where their birthdays fall—they act like I'm someone's kid sister who wandered into the wrong class, a tagalong. The only one who treats me consistently like I belong here is Margot.

When Margot and I first met, we were an unlikely pair. She's one of the kids in my class who is two years older than me. Connecticut has a birthday cutoff date of December 31 for each grade, but sometimes if a kid has a fall birthday, parents will opt to start the kid in school later rather than earlier, which explains how I'm twelve but my best friend in the same grade is fourteen. Not only that, but where I've always been short for my age—short for any age—she's always been incredibly tall.

The first day of third grade, she kept as far away from me as possible. I guess she was thinking that the closer she stood to me, the taller she'd look, which I suppose is correct. But then picture-taking day came, and for some perverse reason our teacher made us stand side by side for the shot. I could see how upset that made Margot, like the teacher was doing it on purpose just to get her. Trying to lighten the moment, when the photographer was almost ready to snap the pic, I whispered in her ear, "Slouch."

"What?" she said, the first word she'd ever spoken to me.

"*Slouch*," I said again, making sure I stressed it this time.

I could tell she had no idea what I was getting at—Margot can be a bit slow on the uptake at times—but I could also tell she responded to the commanding tone of my voice, because slouch she did. At that very second, the very same moment the photographer clicked the shot, I rose up as high as I could on my toes, giving a little jump at the last second. And that's how our third-grade class picture came out: with Margot and me looking the same height but with me being something of a blur, since I was in motion at the time. Margot still didn't talk to me for two weeks afterward, not realizing what my smooth move had achieved. But then the class pics came back. Margot was tickled.

"I look . . . *normal*," she said with a big smile.

"You're a blur," Nana Anna complained. "I can barely tell it's you. It's like you're a shooting star. The school should redo these."

"Um, they only redo individual student pictures that come out cruddy," I pointed out, "not whole class pictures with shooting stars."

Nana Anna may have been displeased, but Margot was looking at me like I could be the best friend she'd been waiting for all her life—and our best friendship was cemented when I embarrassed our hated English teacher by being smarter than him.

"He *so* didn't know *The Lion, the Witch and the Wardrobe* was an allegory until you told him," she said, laughing.

"I know." I laughed back. "Can you believe it?"

But the rest of the kids in our class?

Where Margot found my intelligence a plus because it meant I could help her with her homework if need be, the rest of the kids found my intelligence an insult.

It was as though they were always collectively saying, "Get. Out. First we have to have some shrimpy pip-squeak as a class tagalong, and *now* she has the nerve to be smarter than we are?"

And it didn't help, it *really* didn't help, that during fourth grade, my second year with them as a class, my eighth on this swiftly tilting planet, I started budding breasts.

Mind you, these weren't like the budding breasts you find on girls (and some boys) who eat a steady diet of fast food with a whole box of Stove Top stuffing for a chaser. These were budding breasts on a thin kid. These were "on her way to becoming stacked" budding breasts. My guess is that if we weren't best friends already, Margot would never have forgiven me the sin of starting to develop before any other girl in our class.

The other girls in our class still haven't forgiven me! Yes, it took my breasts two years to arrive at their full flowering at the age of ten, and the other girls— at least most of them—have now caught up, since they're all thirteen and fourteen. But their breasts, not to get too technically weird about it, have that just-barely-done look, like it's something new they have to get used to, like I did at age eight, nine, ten. Whereas mine? They look like I've had them all my life, the way women look when you see them on TV or in magazines.

The girls in my class are so not over me developing first.

And I'm still not over it.

As for the boys?

Oh, are they not over it.

"Torpedoes."

"Bazooms."

"Balloons."

"Kn—"

If you were here from the beginning, I need go no further: You get the idea.

When we were younger, it was as though no one in the history of the world but me had ever acquired breasts. Sometimes I felt like saying, "Hey! You've all got mothers, some of you even have sisters—this shouldn't be anything new!"

Margot's father is a cop, and Mrs. Browning always jokes about him liking to say, "Women want me, men want to *be* me," after a particularly rough weekend on the job, like when some drunk driver pukes all over him or something. One time when she took me and Margot shopping for back-to-school supplies, we ran into some guys in our class at the mall and Mrs. Browning heard some of the comments they made about me. She waited tactfully until Margot was in the bathroom before saying to me, "You know that thing I always tell you girls Margot's father says? Well, it's like that for you, only in reverse: Men want you, women want to *be* you. Or I guess maybe you should substitute 'boys' and 'girls' in there." Then she enveloped me in a big hug. "Oh, honey, I feel for you. It can't be easy." And all the while I was thinking, *Great. The person I share most in common with is a cop who gets puked on.*

The weird thing was, the other girls in our class all wore their white blouses and sweater-vests as tight as they could get away with, as though advertising what they'd recently acquired. Even Margot tried to stuff one summer, but she gave it up when a pair of pantyhose became a floater out of her bikini top after she executed a perfect swan dive off the high board at a classmate's birthday party. Me, I still wore everything loose and my blazer even on the warmest of days to deflect as much attention as possible.

And now here's Margot walking toward me with her notebook clasped to her still-flat chest, hooking up with me outside our lockers. She's practically bouncing, her brown ponytailed hair bouncing along with her. Margot, like so many of our classmates, suffers from "A New School Year, a Brand-New Start" syndrome. Her smile is so infectious, I feel myself pulled along by her hopeful enthusiasm. In fact, I'm just on the verge of bubbling at her—something along the lines of, "You're right! This year will be different! I can just feel it!"—when Fred Johnson brushes past us, making sure his elbow thrusts out far enough to both dislodge Margot's notebook from her protective grasp *and* clip me briefly on the side of the boob.

"Browning—still flat as a board," he observes, "Underwire—still loaded to launch. All's right at Wainscot, and Wainscot's all right with the world."

Margot doesn't even wait for Fred to pass out of earshot before letting loose with the longest string of swear words I've ever heard her utter. Then she turns to me. "Call your grandmother and have her let my mom pick you and me up after school today and drop us at the mall. If the school year's just going to be the lousy same old, same old, at least we can salvage the first day by going shopping."

Sounds like a plan.

MRS. BROWNING PICKS US UP AFTER
school in her Mini Cooper convertible with the
top down. The car is bright blue with white racing
stripes up the middle and white leather seats. I love
this car and only wish I were old enough to drive it.
In a world of SUV moms, Mrs. Browning is a mom
in a class all by herself.

"Good first day?" she asks, the wind whipping
her long brown hair as she puts the car in gear and
zips out of the Wainscot parking lot, going faster
than the posted speed limit. I'm not saying speeding
is cool, but Mrs. Browning is not only a non-SUV
mom, she is also the definition of *cool mom*. She's as
tall as Margot's five feet ten but doesn't wear it like a
burden. Instead, she walks tall and even wears heels,

often reminding Margot that the two most famous women of the last century were also that height—Jacqueline Kennedy Onassis and Princess Diana—and they even both had big feet . . . just like Margot and Mrs. Browning! "Both women hated their feet," Mrs. Browning tells Margot, sometimes as much as once a week, "but look where those feet got them!"

"Dead?" Margot will deadpan.

"Eventually," Mrs. Browning will say with an uncomfortable shrug. "But look where those feet got them before that! They *went* places!"

But Margot never buys it. Margot is convinced that no matter how much she has in common with her gorgeous mother—height, impossibly long legs, beautiful long brown hair, warm brown eyes that make you feel as though they care, and perfect smiles that thumb their noses at orthodontists everywhere—what works so well for her mother will never work for her. Plus, Mrs. Browning has perfect 36C breasts.

"Good first day?" Mrs. Browning asks again.

"Sorry," Margot says from the front seat. Then she jerks her thumb toward me in the backseat. "I thought you were asking her."

Several years ago Mrs. Browning read a book, in

preparation for one day having a teenager, called *Get Out of My Life, But First Could You Drive Me & Cheryl to the Mall.* She swore to herself she'd never be a chauffeur mom, and as soon as we were big enough by state law to sit up front, she always insisted we take turns.

"Well?" Mrs. Browning prompts.

"Define 'good,'" says Margot.

"Oh, dear," Mrs. Browning says, in one of her occasional lapses into TV Mom-dom. "That bad?" With a sigh of relief, she pulls into the mall, conveniently located not far from Wainscot, and drops us off at the Macy's entrance.

Margot is out of the car almost before it stops, and I hand her out her backpack and mine before crawling out of the backseat.

"What time shall I pick you up?" asks Mrs. Browning.

"You're not going shopping?" Margot asks.

"No. I want to get home and start dinner. I'm thinking of doing something with shrimp."

That sounds great to me. Nana Anna tends to favor serving heavy Dutch food, and I've looked at more than one bratwurst in my life.

Margot scrunches her face up at the sky as though reading the moving finger of the sun. While she's doing this, I look at my watch. We get out of school at three fifteen, so it's three thirty now.

"How about six?" Margot suggests.

"Will you have enough time to do your homework?" Mrs. Browning asks.

Margot snorts. It's at moments like that I always catch Mrs. Browning looking at Margot as though her daughter might at any moment turn into a Cheryl. "First day of school, right?" Margot snorts again. "The only advantage is no homework. All *that* fun starts tomorrow."

The mall in the hours after school is like one big party. Kids from the city and the surrounding towns all congregate here, taking over ownership from the Stroller Club moms who rule the shops and food court the rest of the time. Kids get loud here, really loud, much louder than they get during the daytime. It's like they've suddenly been, well, let out of school.

Too bad it doesn't feel as though Margot and I were invited to the party.

We see lots of Wainscot kids here, all kinds of kids

from all kinds of schools, but we're as invisible here as we sometimes feel at Wainscot. What is wrong with us? Do we have signs over our heads that say DON'T BOTHER, CUZ WE'RE LOSERS?

"Want to go to Claire's and try on sunglasses?" Margot suggests.

It seems like a crazy time of year to be trying on sunglasses, despite how hot it is out, plus if Margot wanted to be really cool we'd go to Sunglass Hut, not Claire's, but Sunglass Hut is too expensive and anyway, at least this is something to do.

We're standing just inside the entrance to Claire's and Margot is trying on these retro Wayfarers. I can tell she's not sure about them, but I think they actually look pretty okay on her and I'm about to tell her this when Patty and Deanna stroll by.

"Dork," Patty says.

"Dweeb," Deanna comments.

"Who would ever buy sunglasses like that?" says Patty.

"I'm getting these," Margot suddenly tells me, defiant.

"I think I need a pair too," I say, feeling the familiar rush of sisterly solidarity.

And so there we are five minutes later, twenty dollars poorer each, strutting down the center of the mall like there's a movie soundtrack playing somewhere, Wayfarers on even though we're inside and it's always kind of dark inside the mall.

"*Dude*," Margot says, still strutting, "mocha swirl latte at Dunkin' Donuts?"

"You're on," I say, the epitome of new cool, "but can I get a doughnut, too?"

We sit in the food court, sipping our giant coffee drinks that are more milkshake than coffee, the sun beating through the skylights creating a greenhouse effect. At least it feels like one beneath my blouse, sweater-vest, and blazer. And at least the sunglasses keep the glare from hurting my eyes.

"Dude, aren't you sweltering in that thing?" Margot asks. Margot shed her own blazer as soon as we stepped in the mall. And she never had a sweater-vest on to begin with, so with her sleeves rolled up now, she looks cool—as in cool-in-this-insanely-hot-mall cool—in her white cotton.

And it *is* insanely hot in the mall, the temperature dictated—ridiculously, I might add—by something so arbitrary as the date on the calendar. The air-conditioning goes on March 1, even if there's a blizzard out. It comes off September 1 and the heat goes on, even if it's ninety degrees out like today. This makes absolutely no sense unless the man who owns the mall has never set foot in Connecticut and only read about the state in a book.

"Dude," I say, "uh, *no*. And if you keep calling me 'dude' every sentence? I'm leaving and never coming back."

I break open my doughnut. It's chocolate cream-filled, my favorite, but I can tell from the hardness of the powdered exterior that it's been on the shelf since morning, so I slowly lick out the insides, determined to leave the rest. Meanwhile, Margot bites right into her jelly doughnut, which looks like they just made it. What a world. Chocolate cream-filled doughnuts should always be the most popular, and thus the most fresh.

"Fine," Margot says, "Friend Whom I Will No Longer Call Dude. Time for the postmortem?"

Postmortem is what we do every year after the first day of school: talking about classes, teachers, which kids have changed over the summer, who's hot, and why we're not. There are thirty kids in the eighth grade, divided into two sections. Some classes Margot and I have together—English and history and French—and some we don't, like math and science and art. Everyone takes gym together.

"I'm so glad," Margot says, "that Schrum left before we had to take her. Aren't you?"

She's talking about Beatrice Schrum, of course, who taught U.S. history to the eighth grade at Wainscot for the past forty-two years. She was rumored to take her subject way too seriously, going into fits whenever new tidbits about history came to light, causing her to revise her curriculum. Rumor has it those fits involved tears and flying objects. It's tough, though, to get rid of people with tenure.

"Definitely," I reply, "but I do think it's pretty cool what she's doing instead."

"Agreed. Who knew she dreamed of teaching rhinos to speak?"

"Well," I go on, "at least her replacement, Mr. Parkhurst, doesn't seem to take his subject too seriously, so I think we're safe from flying globes."

"True," she says. "Moving on. Let's see . . . who else do we have together this year? Oh, right. Mr. Dreamy."

"Who?"

"The new English teacher?" she says, like I'm dense. Wainscot has had a lot of teacher turnover lately. "The one *we've* got this year because *we're* so smart?"

She's talking about Robert Fitzgerald, whom I've heard some of the other girls in our class already nickname Mr. FitzDreamy. Where do people come up with these things? Not that he's not good-looking; he really is, for a teacher, with longish dark hair and blue eyes. But he looks like he's barely old enough to teach, and the gossip mill says this is his first year, that he just got his diploma. Still, one day down and he hasn't broken into tears or thrown the globe at a student in posttraumatic stress hysteria over the partitioning of the former USSR—which I guess he wouldn't anyway, since he's the new English teacher, not the new U.S. history teacher—so there is that. But there's something about him, maybe it was his wearing jeans, even if they were neat jeans, when no one else on the Wainscot faculty has, like, *ever*? Maybe I just don't like it when teachers dress too cool? Maybe I expect them to look more like, well, teachers? Maybe I'm a closet conservative?

"He was okay, I guess," I say.

"Okay," she says, obviously miffed at my not being more impressed with her FitzDreamy, "then what about Liam Schwartz?"

"Now him I did notice." And I did. He had two things going for him: He was cute and he was brand-spanking-new. Liam had previously gone to private school in New York City—how cool is that?—and he was taller than the other boys in our class, most of whom were still shorter than Margot, and he had dirty-blond hair, brown eyes, and an easy smile.

The brand-spanking-new part was a plus because, as Margot and I have often lamented, we've known the guys in our class—all fourteen of them—since they were six years old, when they used to still pick their noses when they thought no one was looking or grabbed their crotches if they really had to go to the bathroom bad. It's impossible to picture ever actually dating one of them, now that we're all old enough to have dating on our minds. It'd be like dating your brothers, brothers you didn't really like—euww, euww, double euww! But this new Liam Schwartz presented possibilities . . . for someone.

But probably not for me.

"You can have him," I tell Margot, shrugging magnanimously. It's easy to be generous when you know your chances are nil because—wait for it:

"Well, if it isn't Lacey Under*wire*," I hear.

It's Fred, who's with John and Liam. All of them have street clothes on, as do most of the Wainscot kids I've seen since we've been here. I guess they were all smart enough to change before coming to the mall. I wish I'd been that smart. I feel like such a dork right now, sweltering in my blazer.

"Underwire?" There's a puzzled frown on Liam's face. He nods in our direction and gives a wave as all three walk by. "I thought they said her name was Lacey Underhill when they took attendance."

"Oh, it's Underwire all right." Fred laughs a nasty laugh, and just before they get completely out of earshot I hear, "Did you notice the . . ." I can't hear the end of the sentence, but I don't need my twenty-twenty eyesight to see Fred hold his palms up toward his chest, jiggling them as though weighing two cantaloupes at the supermarket.

"See what I mean?" I say to Margot, forcing a bright smile. "He's all yours. I can't imagine he'd ever be interested in me now."

Margot's face is red. "I don't know why they do that," she says hotly.

"Which part?" I say, suddenly tired.

"That Lacey Underwire stuff, always with the Lacey Underwire. What ever started them on that?" She says the words with great emotion, as though speaking up for my honor, but her eyes shift around and she looks uncomfortable, the way people who aren't used to lying look when they try to lie.

This is a good time for me to get up from the table and toss the wax paper with my doughnut remains and my coffee cup in the trash.

"Who knows?" I say, as if it doesn't really bother me in the slightest.

But the truth is, I do know, and so does Margot, even though Margot doesn't know that I know.

After that birthday party where she lost her pantyhose boobs in the pool, Margot was so embarrassed she'd have done almost anything to get back whatever cool she had. It was then that I overheard her telling some of the other girls in our class about her mother being the one to take me shopping for my first bra and how it was an underwire. Well, of course the girls she told turned around and told everyone else. Selling a friend, a *best* friend, down the river for social currency—what a slippery slope. Still, Margot *was* my best girlfriend, is *still* my best girlfriend, and I'd bet anything that if she could take that sellout back, she'd do so. Heck, most of the time when people say it to me, she looks more upset about it than I do. Maybe it's the guilt.

"So, *dude*," I say, trying to lighten the moment, peering at her over the top of my Wayfarers, "Video World?"

Margot and I are both the kind of geeks who will, if given half a chance, play video games or pinball until carpal tunnel syndrome sets in. I know all about carpal tunnel syndrome, which is basically pain caused by overusing your wrists, because Nana Anna frequently has bouts, only in her case it's from crazy housecleaning, not crazy arcade games.

The sun in Margot's smile comes out again, making me glad I don't keep a grudge. "You're on," she says, looking at me over her own Wayfarers.

We push our sunglasses back up the bridges of our noses and cross the food court, entering Video World. But once we're inside that emporium of noise and occasional flashing lights, it's just too dark to keep the sunglasses on, so Margot tosses hers in her backpack while I shove mine up on my head.

"Ms. Pac-Man?" she suggests hopefully. Any day Margot can get to the screen where she gets to eat the yellow banana, worth five thousand points, she's happy.

"Nah," I say. I don't want to disappoint her, but hey, if we're best friends, we should each get to play the game we most want to play, right? "I'm in the mood for pinball."

As she makes her way over to her game of choice, I head off to the Lord of the Rings pinball machine, relieved to find it empty. Not that there's usually much competition for it. Most of the kids who come in here prefer the fast pace of the simulated cars and motorcycles and fighter planes, leaving the field free for me and Margot to indulge our taste for more old-fashioned games, some of them—like Ms. Pac-Man—going back all the way to the days when our parents were in school.

The Lord of the Rings pinball machine isn't *that* old, but even if it were, I'd still love playing it, and I'm feeling that love as I work through my first silver ball and then my second of three. I'm mid-second ball when in my peripheral vision I catch sight of a hand putting two quarters in the corner of the slanted glass top of the machine. Hey, what gives? Quarters on the machine: the classic pinball or video player's sign that he or she is calling the next game. And there's something about the fleeting glimpse I get of that hand as it moves away, its owner standing behind me, perhaps so as not to distract, that tells me the hand's owner is male . . . *very* male, like maybe even *manly*, meaning the owner's hand is nothing like the hands of, say, Fred or John or even Liam, which are still boys' hands.

But I push that possibly interesting fact aside as I get lost in playing that second ball. My goal right now? To get the Balrog to light up red. He's in the middle of the screen, and when he lights up, he'll do a one-eighty turn and then wonderful, magical things will happen: The machine will go bonkers and all the extra balls it's been storing for me as I've been racking up the points on this one ball will be released. Something like four balls will come at me at once, and it will be my job to keep them all in play at the same time.

It happens. I get the Balrog to turn, and suddenly

I'm playing for my life, it feels like, jamming the flippers to beat the band, that last being something Nana Anna says, only not in relation to pinball. I keep it going as long as I can, knowing without looking up at the counter that I'm now racking up millions upon millions of points. If I'm lucky, I'll get the thirteen million needed for a free game— a rare feat. But there's only so long my wrists can keep doing this, much as I like to sometimes believe I can do it forever, and I watch as one, two, and then three balls are lost. I still have that last one going when it comes down the far left, heading straight for the gutter lane. I put my hip into it and jiggle the machine with just the right amount of finesse, caus- ing the ball to stay in play rather than guttering out, but *without* tilting the machine. I keep it going for another fifteen seconds, giving it simultaneous full hip action with a strong slam on the flippers to save it, but two seconds later the gutter finally gets me.

I'm almost scared to look at the counter as I hear the bonus points click in, but when I do I see I'm at twelve million and change. So close and still one ball to go. I can *do* this. Even though my wrists are killing me—screaming, actually—I can do this.

I don't give myself time to rest, to second-guess myself. I pull back hard on the spring-controlled device that sends the last ball hurtling toward my victory, and it's then I hear a velvety but masculine voice behind me say, with full admiration, "Wow, you're good."

I don't know why I do it. I'm a pinball wizard. I know the importance of keeping my eye on the prize. But I turn at the sound of that voice to see the speaker and, oh *man*, is he gorgeous!

Then I tear myself away, turn back to my game just in time to see my last ball go straight down the center gutter between the two now-useless flippers. Game over. I look at the counter and see that, even though I didn't do anything, the machine tallies me an extra five thousand points on the ball, kind of like a token for just showing up, like when our French teacher gives us two points extra on tests just for remembering to put our French names correctly on the little line at the top of the page: a gimme. But even if the machine is generous enough to give me something for doing nothing, it's still not enough to get me up to the thirteen-million-point place where I want to be. And so another dream dies.

But there are new dreams!

I turn around to face the reason I lost my pinball dream. My previous impression of general gorgeousness is confirmed—he's nothing like Fred or John or even Liam, nothing like any of the boys in my eighth-grade class at Wainscot. He's taller than the boys in my class, but that's not it. It's how he wears that height and strength, like he's comfortable inside it, like it's nothing new to him. His jeans hang low on his hips, more ratty than Wainscot guys would ever wear, even on Messy Art Days. There's something about him that says he really did go to the concert mentioned on the dark T-shirt he's wearing instead of, like, buying it just so people would think he's cool, even though he's never seen the band at all. And his hair! Wainscot guys aren't allowed to wear their hair that long, at least not in middle school, a fact that always makes me want to fight with the school board, because aren't we supposed to be all about freedom of expression? (Well, except for the uniforms, which is the height of conformity even if they push it at us as some sort of social-equality thing.) But none of that matters right now. Because that hair is a deep auburn color! And I swear his eyes are the same, as though they're some kind of brick-tinted brown. And, oh, is that real stubble on his chin?

"I'm so sorry," he's saying.

"Hmm?" I say intelligently, exercising all of my high-IQ points as I tilt my head to meet his eyes.

"I'm sorry," he repeats, and now what he's saying is starting to register and I can see he's sincere. "I screwed up your game. I couldn't help it, though. I've never seen a girl, I've hardly ever seen *anyone* play that machine like that. You were just so great, I had to say something."

"Er, thanks." I'm just one step away from hitting myself on the side of the head for all my inarticulate idiocy. Where are all my smooth words from books? Where are those sonnets I've memorized? I could recite a sonnet right now!

Thank God I don't recite a sonnet.

"Here," he says, taking his quarters off the machine, then taking my hand, pressing the quarters into it because I'm in mannequin mode, folding my fingers over the quarters for me since I can't seem to snap *out* of mannequin mode. *Man*, his hand feels good. "You take my game. You deserve to play again."

At last—praise the universe!—I find my voice again, my real voice.

"Thanks, but I can't," I say, trying to push the quarters from my palm back into his palm.

"But you have to," he insists. "It's only fair."

"But I can't," I tell him. I remove my hand from his with regret, holding up my wrists. "They've practically gone carpal tunnel on me," I explain. "I'm done for the day."

He gets a wistful look on his face, like he would have really liked to see me play some more, but then he takes the quarters back and puts them in the slot. "Watch me play?" he asks. "For luck?"

I'm still nodding like a bobblehead toy when Margot comes up.

"Hey," she says, "Dance-A-Holic is free. Wanna dance?"

Outside of the retro video games and pinball machines, Dance-A-Holic is our favorite thing to do here. It's a really loud music machine with psyche-delic flashing colors that light up on the platform you stand on, indicating where to put your feet. Margot and I like to practice our smooth dance moves on it. Neither of us ever says, but I think each time we do it we're privately imagining we're at a school dance somewhere, dancing with the kind of guy who could have "Dreamy" suffixed at the end of his name. Perhaps today Margot will imagine she's dancing with Liam SchwartzDreamy?

But I tell her no. "I was just about to watch"—I look at him because I realize I don't even know his name—"*him* play a round of Lord of the Rings."

"Him" holds out his hand to Margot, correcting the lapse. "Chad Wilcox," he says, and I see he gives her hand a firm grip.

Hey! I think. *Haven't we skipped a step here? Shouldn't he be shaking my hand?* Still, Chad Wilcox sounds like the most perfect name, like, *ever.*

"Charmed, I'm sure," Margot says in her best private-school fashion, but she drops his hand quickly as though she's done with him. She turns to me. "Are you sure you don't want to dance?"

I bobblehead again.

"Okay, then," she says, walking away reluctantly.

Chad takes a big breath. "Ready?" he says, as if he's actually nervous for some reason about playing a game that, based on his interest in watching me play, he's probably played a lot.

"Here goes nothing!" I say brightly, because I can't think of anything better and it's something Nana Anna always says. But what does "Here goes nothing!" mean exactly? It sounds so stupid when I say it out loud. Shouldn't it be "Here goes something"? Who wants "nothing" to happen when they're about to do something important? And why am I obsessing about this so much? Maybe I should have just said, "Knock 'em dead," giving him a playful jab on the shoulder?

But Chad doesn't seem to notice my awkwardness or my interior obsession with aphorisms, because he just smiles, says "Thanks," and pulls the spring-activated device all the way back to shoot his first silver ball into the upper regions of Lord of the Rings.

I watch him play, forgetting for a moment he's *him*. And I'm pleasantly surprised to see how good he is. What was I expecting him to be, as Nana Anna would say, chopped liver? As he racks up points with his first ball, I see him play the machine with as much authority as I do, repeatedly jiggling the table enough to keep the ball in play while avoiding the dreaded tilt before finally guttering out at five million points.

He turns to me with a rueful grin. "I'm pretty sure you scored more than that on your first ball."

Right now I frankly can't remember if I did or not, but I like it that, despite the rueful grin, he doesn't look upset at being bested by a Girl. And I *really* like it that he's so good on my favorite machine. Would I like him less if he wasn't? I'd like to think no, but it definitely helps, how good he is.

He's about to let the second ball fly when he turns to me and gets a look on his face like he's just noticed something.

"Hey," he says, "aren't you hot in here in that jacket?"

And I *am* hot. I feel like I'm in the witch's oven from *Hansel and Gretel*, having worked up a sweat playing Lord of the Rings, practically turning it into a contact sport. But I don't usually take off my camouflage in front of boys. Then I think: But Chad seems so much more mature than the boys I know—surely he won't be totally flummoxed by something as silly as 36C breasts, will he?

Slowly, feeling a blush of shyness cover my face, I take off my blazer. Then, something in the act of finally taking off my blazer makes me realize just exactly how hot I am, and I follow that brave act by pulling my oversize sweater-vest over my head as well, being careful to hold down my white blouse with one hand so it doesn't ride up and . . . show things.

"That's better." Chad smiles a relieved smile, which is very nice; at least he doesn't look like he's going to go into convulsions over a silly thing like breasts or start making up obnoxious names for them. "I was beginning to get hot just looking at you."

His face is innocent, and somehow I don't think he realizes how that sounds.

Then he gives my body an appreciative once-over, and the weird thing is that, unlike the obnoxious way the guys at school look at my body, his once-over just makes me feel, well, appreciated. And attractive. That too.

"Did you forget about your game?" I say, feeling the blush that reddens my cheeks again.

"I guess I did," he says, and there's another great smile.

Wow, all this smiling. I swear he's smiled more times at me in the last ten minutes, nicely, than all the boys in the world have in the last two years. I start wondering how old he is. Definitely older than me. I mean, *duh*. But how much older? Fourteen? Fifteen? How old do you have to be to have genuine stubble on your chin that you might actually have to shave off every day?

My first older guy. My first guy!

"So, um," I say, "maybe you should play your second ball?"

"Right."

While he's working the second ball, I steal my eyes away long enough to glance over to see how Margot's doing. She's still on Dance-A-Holic, but she looks like she's getting tired. I would be too if I'd been on it as long as she has. I look back to see how Chad is doing and see the second ball disappear down the side lane. I check the counter and notice he's now at just a little more than twelve million, right where I was after ball two, needing just one more million to win a freebie.

He turns around and reaches out a hand. "Here," he says, indicating the blazer and sweater I've draped over my arm, "let me take those for you. You shouldn't have to carry everything."

Before I can ask what's up, he takes the clothing

items and drapes them over his left arm. Then, with his right hand, body still turned toward me, eyes still on me, he reaches behind himself and pulls the spring-action thingy, putting the last ball into play. He doesn't even look at the ball, but I do. I watch in horrified fascination as it pings around the interior of the machine and bounces off the flippers a few times before slowly rolling through the center gutter. With no one playing the flippers, it's just the law of gravity catching up with the ball. The ball has no choice but to eventually go dead.

"What are you, *crazy*?" I say. "You had it. You had it. It would have been so easy. All you needed was just a million more points to go over the top. What were you *thinking* of?"

"You," he answers, and now there's a smile that's somehow different from the ones that have come before. "I was responsible for distracting you from beating the machine on your own game, right? It wouldn't be fair for me to take my own win."

Omi*god*! Is he cute, or what?

I can't even say anything, I'm smiling so wide.

"Um," he says, "isn't this the place where you finally tell me your name?"

"It's Lacey," I say, might as well get the worst over with now, "Lacey Underhill."

"I like it," he says, after a moment's consideration. "Underhill—isn't that the name Bilbo Baggins uses as an alias in *The Hobbit*? Mr. Underhill?"

Omigod—a guy who can make a literary reference *and* gets that this is thematic, given that we just met over the Lord of the Rings game and all.

"Yes," I say. "Yes, it is."

"So," he says slowly, "your name is Lacey Underhill and you're a Wainscot girl."

Even in my mentally compromised state, compromised by his gorgeousness, I know he deduces this because of my uniform. The Wainscot uniform is very distinctive, and all students wear the same uniform, K–12.

"Yes," I say intelligently.

"So, Lacey Underhill, what year are you in?"

What *year* am I in? Hold the phones. He must think that I, at all of twelve years, am in high school. If he thought I was still in grade school, he'd ask, "What grade are you in?" instead.

"Ohhhh, you know," I say, practically shuffling my feet, "one of those years with a number in it."

I'm saved from answering further questions about my educational achievement status because Margot is back. Thank *God* she got tired of the dance machine at just the right time.

"I think we need to get going," she tells me. Then she looks at me and frowns. "You took your jacket off! And your vest!"

I scowl at her. I don't want Chad to think I'm some kind of geek who wears, like, six layers of clothes when it's hot. "I. Got. Hot." I practically bite out the words through gritted teeth, forcing a smile at the same time.

"Can I give you ladies a lift somewhere?" Chad offers.

And that's when it hits me: He's not fourteen or even fifteen—he's sixteen! He has to be if he's offering us a lift. He must go to the local high school, since he doesn't go to Wainscot, and . . . and he drives! And shaves!

"No, thanks," Margot starts to say, "my mo—"

But I cut her off. How uncool would it be for him to know her *mother* is our ride? "Margot's my lift, so I think I'd better go with her. After all, you know what Frank Sinatra always says."

"No," Chad says, "what does he say?"

Damn Nana Anna for always listening to those stupid old records!

"Um," I say, "I think he says something about always leaving with the one you came with."

"That sounds like a good philosophy," Chad says, considering. "But don't you think he's probably talking about *dates*? You know, like romantic dates?"

"Um . . ." I can't believe some guy said the word "dates" with me in the room, not that I think he's asking me out on one or anything, or that he would ask me out on one. Will anyone ever ask me out on one?

"C'mon," Margot says to me, getting visibly antsy. "We gotta go." She takes my blazer and sweater out of Chad's hands and hands them back to me, picks my backpack off the floor, and shoves it into my arms. Now she's actually pulling on my arm.

"Uh, bye," I shout, now practically halfway to the door.

"Can I call you sometime?" he shouts after me.

"Uh, sure!" I shout back.

"But how will I—"

And we're gone.

THE REST OF THE WEEK GOES BY AND
I spend my time doodling in my notebooks.

Okay, I don't spend *all* my time doodling—I also
do the normal stuff like brush my teeth and take
showers; sometimes I even eat.

I write "Chad Wilcox" in something like a hundred—a thousand?—variations on the inside covers
of my math and science notebooks.

You wouldn't think there'd be so many different
ways to write out "Chad Wilcox," but I manage it. I use
different-colored pens, pencils, and markers. I turn the
dot on the *i* into various-size hearts. I fill the centers
of the *a*, *d*, and *o* with little smiley faces. And, all the
while, I imagine the "ox" at the very end represents
the universal symbol for "hug, kiss," a nicely cryptic

reversal on the more usual configuration of "xo" for "kiss, hug."

What can I say?

I'm sort of in love. For the first time in my life, I'm sort of in love, and it's with an older guy I met only once but who happens to play a mean game of pinball.

Who could resist?

As the week goes on, I wonder why I doodle my doodlings only inside my math and science notebooks, the classes I don't share with Margot. I leave the notebooks for English and history and French— the classes I do share with her—in their original pristine condition. What is my subconscious trying to tell me? But then Thursday comes, and with it Margot coming by my house after school to do homework and have dinner, and I realize exactly what my subconscious has been trying to tell me.

But first . . .

"What's that smell?" asks Margot as we enter the house, throwing our blazers on the telephone chair in the entryway.

I sniff the air. I'm an expert at sniffing out Nana Anna's cooking.

"Pea soup." I sniff again. "There's bacon and sausage in it too."

"Is it okay," Margot asks, "for me to say that sounds gross?"

"You can say it," I reply with a shrug, "but Nana Anna will still make us eat it. That's dinner you're smelling. Ours."

"We're having pea soup as our whole dinner?" Margot exercises her inquiring mind.

"You'd be surprised how much meat and how many vegetables will be crammed into your soup bowl," I tell her. "And if that's not enough, for a side dish there will be potatoes the size of your head. Or at least something to do with potatoes."

"God," Margot says, "in my house, we'd never get anything like that. My mom's always on, you know"—she rolls her eyes—"South Beach." Then she giggles. "Actually, it smells pretty good. It smells like, you know, real food."

"Girls?" I hear Nana Anna's voice call out from the kitchen.

Sometimes, when I can only hear her but can't see her, I'm surprised at how old she sounds.

"That's us," I yell back. "We're still girls!"

"Do your schoolwork first," says Nana Anna. "Then, we eat."

"I can't wait, Nana Anna!" Margot says. All my friends call my grandmother that. Nana Anna says it's okay to have just one grandchild, and that she likes it like that, but that it's also nice to think about the rest of the world's children all belonging to her somehow. This might seem very witch-in-a-fairy-tale coming from anyone else, but from Nana Anna it's actually somehow cool.

"That pea soup smells like nothing I've ever smelled before!" Margot adds, causing me to punch her on the arm as we giggle our way up the stairs to my room.

Once inside, we change out of our uniforms. Margot has brought jeans and a T-shirt in her backpack, and I put on the same. At Wainscot we're not allowed to wear jeans even on dress-down days, so we wear them outside of school whenever we get the chance.

After we have our favorite clothes on, we get straight down to homework.

This may sound like a boring thing to do, like we should be talking about boys or music instead or something, but Wainscot likes to keep kids' minds sharp with lots of hard work, even at the beginning of the year, and if we don't keep up we'll be lost.

So that's what we're still doing an hour and a half later—Margot's working on her math homework, while I'm mild-manneredly attacking my first English paper of the year—when disaster strikes.

Margot asks if she can borrow some graph paper, saying she forgot hers in her locker at school, and without even thinking about it I say yes.

Not a minute later I hear, "Lacey, what are you, nuts?"

It's not the first time in my life someone has leveled this accusation at me, so I don't grasp the enormity of the situation right away. But then I look up and see what particular thing is causing Margot to question my sanity this time. She's staring at the inside of my math notebook, a look of horror on her face as she takes in all those multicolored variations on "Chad Wilcox."

"Has he even *called* you yet?" she demands.

I shake my head no. "But—"

"*Eet smakelijk!*" Nana Anna calls up from down below.

The first time Margot ate over here, years ago, she was surprised when Nana Anna gave her usual dinner call.

"What's she saying?" Margot asked.

"She's calling us to dinner," I explained. "It's Dutch. It means 'eat deliciously.' Yeah, I know," I added, "it sounds funny, but it's a nice sentiment, isn't it? C'mon, let's wash up."

"Fine," she says now, "but don't think you're going to get off so easily. After dinner, after we *eet smakelijk*, we're going to talk some more. I'm not finished with you yet."

Oh, brother.

"Wow, this is really good," Margot says a few minutes later, surprise in her voice at how much she likes the soup.

"Thank you," Nana Anna says. Then she adds, "Get your left hand out of your lap and stop resting your right elbow on the table."

"Dutch manners," I remind Margot as Nana Anna goes into the kitchen.

Whenever Margot's eaten here before, we've mostly had pizza or burgers or chicken nuggets, but Nana

Anna is laying on the whole Dutch treatment tonight, and for that she demands Dutch manners.

When Nana Anna comes back, she has a platter heaped with what look like the thickest French fries in the world along with two dipping bowls. One has a whitish spread in it, while the other is darker.

"What's this?" Margot asks.

"*Patat*," I say.

"*Patat oorlog*," Nana Anna corrects.

"It means 'French fries war,'" I tell Margot. "The white stuff is mayonnaise, the other stuff is peanut sauce."

"I can see why the potatoes are fighting," says Margot, and I kick her under the table before she can say "gross" again.

I know she'd love to decline this delicacy, but no one ever says no to Nana Anna.

Margot surprises herself again by liking the battling French fries.

"Wow," she says, "this is impressive. I never knew a person could gain, like, ten pounds at one meal."

"*Phtt*," Nana Anna phtts at Margot. "You young girls. You all worry about the diet, the diet—all the time. 'Does this have fat in it?' 'Does this have protein?' 'Does this have carbohydrates?'" She makes a face of disgust at the idiocy that is young girls living in America. "But me, I've been eating this food all my life, and look at me!"

We look.

"Do I look like I'm fat or out of shape?" Nana Anna presses.

"No," I say. "You look strong as a house."

"You look like you could paint a house," Margot adds.

"You look like you could paint one right now," I finish.

"That's right," Nana Anna exclaims, pounding herself on the chest like she's King Kong trying to make a point.

But something about her King Kong routine goes wrong and suddenly she's coughing like she can't catch her breath. I've never seen her cough like this before.

"What is it?" I ask, rushing to her side.

"Should I call 911?" asks Margot, rushing to her other side. "Do you need me to do the Heimlich?"

"No." Nana Anna pats her chest as her body visibly

starts to calm. "My heart hurt for just a minute there, but I'm fine now."

"I still think we should call the doctor," I say. "Do you want me to get your heart medication?"

"No," Nana Anna insists. "I'm fine. I just need some dessert."

"You stay here," Margot offers. "I'll go get it for you. What does it look like?"

"There should be a plate with biscuits on it," says Nana Anna. "The biscuits have blue and white squares on top."

"I'll explain later," I say to Margot's raised eyebrows.

"So, um, what are these?" Margot asks, returning with the platter.

"*Muisjes*," Nana Anna says, rising to serve. She looks so strong now. You'd never guess she was gasping for breath a moment before. It's as if it never happened.

"Mice," I translate for Margot. "Well, of course they're not *real* mice," I add, seeing her horrified expression. "Even *we* don't eat real mice. They're just called that. And they look like that. But they're made with anise and sugar coating."

"My," Margot says, "that sounds so . . . *ethnic.*" But she surprises herself one last time by liking those, too.

"So," Nana Anna declares, "now that I have served you girls a healthy meal, you must tell me: How are things going?"

"Great," I say, the perfect one-word answer.

"*Not,*" Margot corrects, sugar coating building up in the corners of her grim smile. "As a matter of fact, I think Lacey is about to make a huge—"

Mistake, mistake, I just know she's going to say *mistake*! So I do the only thing I can do, because if she says *mistake* Nana Anna will never let us get up from the table until it's fully explained: I kick Margot under the table. Hard.

Over Margot's "Ouch!" I pass the plate of mice to her, taking one for myself first.

"She was about to say," I tell Nana Anna, "that I'm going to make a big fat pig of myself if I keep eating like this. But"—I pop the mouse into my mouth, talking around the biscuit—"who can resist?"

Then, for good measure, I shove a mouse into Margot's gaping mouth.

"C'mon," I say, grabbing her arm and tugging,

knowing she's too insecure about looking gross to talk with food in her mouth. "Thanks for dinner!" I call back to Nana Anna. "I'll do the dishes later!"

Back in my room, the door safely shut, Margot at last swallows her mouse.

"What was that all about?" she demands.

"I can't have you ratting me out to Nana Anna," I say. "I hate keeping secrets from her, but if you tell her I like a boy, she'll want to know all about him, and then you'll tell her he's sixteen and she'll hit the roof."

"Which is exactly my point," she says. "She should be upset about it. *I'm* upset about it!"

"What do you have to be upset about?" I ask, genuinely curious.

"This . . . *Chad* guy is so much older than you, Lacey," she says. "And I'm sure he'd never have shown so much interest in you if it weren't for your . . . *breasts.*"

"*What?*"

"It's true. Why would a sixteen-year-old go for a girl who's so much younger, if it weren't for something like that?"

"But he doesn't know I'm younger!"

"*Exactly*. And the reason he thinks you're older is because your body *tells* him you're older. But you're not."

I think back to the afternoon at the mall. Chad didn't even see my breasts—I mean, not that he ever *saw* them, but he must have gotten some idea of the size of them beneath my white blouse—until after he'd been with me for a while.

"You're wrong," I say with absolute confidence. "Chad liked me for me that day."

"Oh, yeah?" she says. "Then why hasn't he called?"

I'd concede her the point except for one thing: "He *can't* call," I say, "because *you* dragged me out of there before I had the chance to give him my number."

"And it's a very good thing I did that," Margot retorts.

"I can't believe we're having a fight about a boy," I say, trying on a laugh.

But as I say it, I realize I *can* believe it. Margot has always been jealous of me, even though she's never come out and admitted it, which is why she started that whole "Lacey Underwire" thing with the other kids. And now, because of her jealousy, she's trying to convince me that Chad only likes me for my breasts. How small can she be?

But then I realize that I've always been jealous of her, too. I've been jealous of her for having a mom and a dad.

"Look," I say, "whatever you do, please don't say any more about this in front of Nana Anna. It will only get her upset."

"Yeah," Margot admits. "Did you see the way she looked when she was choking at dinner?"

"I did, but nothing bad can happen to Nana Anna."

"How can you be so sure of that?" asks Margot.

"Because if something happened to Nana Anna," I say, "then what would happen to me?"

BUT OF COURSE NOTHING HAPPENS TO Nana Anna.

I wake up the next day, Friday, and go to school, same as usual.

Except that nothing feels the same as usual. All day long, it's as though there's a barrier between me and Margot. It's as though, after our discussion last night, we can't talk to each other anymore.

This makes for a lonely day for me.

When I think about it, I think it must make for a lonely day for Margot as well.

So as we move to leave English class, the whole class upset that Mr. FitzDreamy has assigned another paper to be done over the weekend, I go up to her, figuring I'll be the bigger person.

"Hey," I say, holding my notebook with all its variations of "Chad Wilcox" close to my chest, "why don't I give Nana Anna a call and say your mom is picking both of us up after school today, rather than me taking the bus? Then we could do something together. I mean, even though we have this English assignment to do, it *is* the weekend."

I see Margot's eyes brighten for the first time that day. It's too hard, us not talking to each other. I mean, if we don't have each other to talk to, who will we talk to? Deanna? Patty?

"That's a great idea!" Margot says. "What did you have in mind?"

"I don't know." I look down at the top of my notebook. "I was thinking maybe we could go to the mall?"

I look up in time to see the light go out of her eyes.

"And what did you have in mind for us to do there?" she says in a hard voice.

"I don't know," I say again. I try to look innocent, like I've just now thought of this. "Maybe we could play some video games at Video World?"

"Give me some credit," she says. "The only reason

you want to go to the mall, the only reason you want to play *video games*"—she makes air quotes as she says those last two words, just like Mr. FitzDreamy does all the time—"is because you're secretly hoping we'll run into *Chad*."

"That's not true!" I say with all the outrage I can muster, feeling the flush of embarrassment at being caught redden my cheeks even as I say the words. "I've always liked video games. We both have!"

"Tell you what," she says with a level stare. "How about we go to the mall, but we get our nails done instead. How about we go to the mall, but you promise we won't go anywhere *near* Video World?"

I hold the stare as long as I can. I hold it until I realize we could both do this all day, with no one winning.

"Never mind," I finally say through clenched teeth. "It just occurred to me that this new English assignment is going to be a *bear*. I'd better just go straight home after school and start it right away so I can hand it in on time."

But when I get home from school, I don't go anywhere near my English assignment. There's still plenty of time to get that done, and I have other things on my mind.

"I'll be up in my room until dinnertime!" I shout out to Nana Anna, slamming the door behind me.

"Don't you even come and say hello anymore?" says my grandmother, wiping her hands on her apron as she catches me, halfway up the stairs.

"Oops, sorry," I say, feeling guilty. I go back down the stairs, give her a quick kiss, start again. "Hello! How was your day?"

"It was good. I tamed the garden. How was yours?"

"Good too," I lie, all the while thinking how bad the day was with Margot. I sniff the air. "Mmm . . . spaghetti and meatballs?"

"You got it in one, kiddo. That's some sniffer you have there."

"Is there a reason why we couldn't have had something normal like that when Margot was over last night?"

"What's *normal*?" She shrugs. "So I wanted to give your friend a real meal for once. So sue me."

I practically shuffle my feet. "Well, if that's all . . ."

Nana Anna gives her head a tiny jerk, indicating

the top floor of the house. "What's so important you got to do up there until dinnertime?"

"Um . . . stuff." Before she can say anything else, I give her another quick kiss on the cheek. "See ya!"

This time, I don't just shut the door. I lock it.

Then I have a one-girl fashion show, Lacey Underhill–style.

I've spent my whole life—okay, maybe not my whole life, but at least the last two years, which sometimes feels like my whole life—trying to camouflage my breasts. But now I go through my entire wardrobe, Chad in mind, looking for ways to enhance them. I know I told Margot that Chad doesn't like me for my breasts, and yet her words still ring in my mind:

"*I'm sure he'd never have shown so much interest in you if it weren't for your* breasts. . . . *The reason he thinks you're older is because your body* tells *him you're older. But you're not.*"

I tried to play it cool with Margot at the time, and Chad didn't seem at all like a breastcentric creep that time I met him, but still Margot's words haunt me. What if she's right? And whether she's right or wrong, won't Chad expect a girl he likes to look close to his age? And doesn't that mean breasts and cleavage or, at the very least, showing a shape?

So into my wardrobe I go.

I have loose sweaters for fall and winter, loose sweaters for summer. It's like I own every garment ever invented that doesn't show a silhouette. True, I have a few close-fitting items, things Mrs. Browning got for Margot to give me for birthday and holiday presents, but I've only been daring enough to wear those under my famous loose clothes.

It's those close-fitting items I seek out now.

The first one is not so much close fitting as it is sheer, being a white gauze top with bell sleeves and embroidery around the square neck. I take off my uniform and put the gauze top on over jeans. Then I cover my face with my hands, almost scared to look in the full-length mirror.

When I do, I'm surprised to see it doesn't look awful on me. But I'm also surprised at something else. The material is so sheer, you can see the whole outline of my shape underneath—you can see the color of my skin, you can even see my belly button. You can see straight through this thing to my bra! What was Mrs. Browning thinking of?

Sure, I've worn bathing suits before. Maybe someday I'll even be brave enough to wear a bikini. But there's no way I could ever wear this in public. It's too much like being naked. It's somehow worse than being naked!

I remove the gauze top so quickly, it's as though my imagination is telling me the whole world has X-ray eyes and everyone can somehow see me right now. Once I'm free I consign the offending garment to the bottom of my closet.

What's next?

Hmm . . .

What's next turns out to be a crimson satin blouse. The sleeves end in superwide cuffs, and this one really is close fitting. It has a row of little hidden metal hooks and eyes that come up the front, ending just in the middle of my, um, *cleavage*.

(God, I hate that word.)

But as I put the hooks through the eyes, something feels *right* about this shirt, and this time I don't even take the precaution of covering my eyes before looking at my reflection in the full-length mirror. And, when I do . . .

Wow! I mean, like, wowie-wow-wow!

With just the change of a shirt, I don't even look like me anymore. I look like . . . like the kind of girl a sixteen-year-old guy would want to date.

I look like the kind of girl that a guy like Chad might want to date.

Or just about.

But if I put on some of the makeup we're not allowed to wear at Wainscot until we're in high school and that Nana Anna lets me wear only a little of on very special occasions, like school choral concerts . . . if I put on a little silver eye shadow, like so, and some dark mascara, like so, until—ouch! I poke myself in the eye with the wand. After recovering from my eye injury and wiping away the excess mascara from the corner of the eye I stabbed myself in, I apply some shimmery pink lipstick, like so . . .

"La-cey!" Nana Anna's voice yells up the staircase to me. "You've got a vi-si-tor! It's a bo-oy!"

I'm marveling at her ability to turn the one-syllable "boy" into a two-syllable shout, when all of a sudden I realize:

Boy? Boy? B-b-b-boy? Did Nana Anna say BOY?

Omigod! The magic I've been working up here by

trying on more mature tops and experimenting with makeup has paid off and delivered a magnificent result—it's magically produced a *boy* at my door!

And it must be Chad Wilcox. Somehow he has found the way to my door.

"Coming!" I shout, cursing myself even as I say it for sounding too eager and then cursing myself doubly as I trip over the corner of the area rug, stumbling across the floor in my overeagerness to get to the door and down the stairs. To Chad.

The upstairs hallway is just a hardwood floor—Nana Anna, in her Dutchness, is big on hardwood—and I skid across it, stopping just in time to poke my head around the corner, expecting to see Chad Wilcox looking up at me from down below. But, instead of Chad Wilcox, it's . . .

"Sam Samuels?" I blurt out as I see his three-years-older-than-the-last-time-I-saw-him head, with its familiar black hair. His brown eyes are gazing up at me, and he's got a wide smile.

"Lacey!" he calls up at me, pure joy.

Omigod! I look down at my crimson satin blouse, revealing all of my proud cleavage. I can't let Sam Samuels see me looking like this! I look sixteen!

"I'm, um, not decent yet," I stutter, then force a bright grin. "Back in a flash!"

And I disappear.

Sam Samuels was my sandbox buddy, my best friend when I was younger. I know I said Margot is my best friend, and she *is* my best friend . . . at Wainscot. Plus she's my best girlfriend. But Sam Samuels was my best neighborhood friend and my best overall friend since I was in diapers. His family moved in down the street when I was five months old. Even though he's nearly two years older than me—just like Margot, Sam's in the same grade as me, but because he has a fall birthday and I'm a year ahead, there's still a big age difference—when I said "goo," he humored me by saying "gah," and the rest is history.

As we grew a bit older, even when he started in the public school system while I later attended Wainscot, we remained best friends. We stuck up for each other.

The year I started kindergarten, there was a bully in the neighborhood whose name was Steve Lancer and who thought Sam's name was something to laugh at, particularly since back then Sam went by Sammy.

"Sammy Samuels," Steve sneered one day in a girly voice. "What kind of doofus name is that? Were your parents so stupid they couldn't think of anything better than to give you most of your last name for your first?"

"His name is Sam," I said, instantly giving my best friend a more boy-sounding name, adding the epithet, "poopyhead."

Then I blew raspberries at Steve until he finally walked away in disgust. All those raspberries made my lips feel numb, like I'd been kissing a power drill or something, but I like to think they were instrumental in causing Steve's family to move out of state later that month.

Lacey and Sam, Sam and Lacey.

We watched TV at each other's houses, read comic books together, played outside and got dirty in a way I was never allowed to at Wainscot, watched horror movies on Saturday nights while Nana Anna napped on the sofa.

And then, when I was nine, Sam's father got transferred to Chicago and they moved away. We said we'd keep in touch and we did, in the beginning. But he never came back to visit, I never had reason to go to Chicago, and eventually that petered out.

So Sam, my sandbox buddy, the boy I'd been a tomboy with for the first nine years of my life, had missed the bulk of my mammary flowering altogether.

But now he was back, at least for today.

And I wanted to go back too: back to that time in my life when things were so simple, when the most complex decision in my world involved which comic book to read or which rude thing to say to defend against Steve Lancer.

I just couldn't let Sam see me like this.

In my room, I tear the crimson satin blouse off so quickly that I'm lucky it's held together with hooks and eyes; buttons would have torn right off, scattering all over the room.

Then I quickly throw on my largest sweatshirt: an orange one. Camouflage in place, I wipe off as much of the makeup as I can and straighten out my hair before heading back downstairs in what I hope is a nonchalant stroll.

"I was just telling Nana Anna how great the house looks all pink like this," Sam tells me as I hit the bottom stair.

"And I was telling him," Nana Anna says, "it's always been this pink."

"I guess I just forgot all of its, um, *pinkness* when I was away," Sam says with a smile.

It's a nice smile, and it's only after I've looked at him for a moment now that we're up close—taking in that he's grown a little taller since I last saw him but that, always having been kind of short, he's still only a bit taller than me—that I notice that his voice has changed. He doesn't squeak anymore like he sometimes did before he went away. I wonder if he's still surprised sometimes when he hears the sound of his new voice, just like I'm still surprised sometimes when I wake up in the morning to find I still have big breasts and it's not all a dream—or a nightmare.

"It's good to see you, Lacey," he says. "I really missed you."

I punch him lightly on the shoulder, guy-style. "So, how long are you here for—the weekend?"

"For good," Sam says, adding, "or at least for now. My dad got transferred back. He bought our old house."

And then the phone rings.

7.

SAM SAMUELS IS BACK HOME AGAIN
for good.

Omigod, I can't believe it! This is going to be
so excellent. We can go back to doing everything
together exactly the way we used to. I'm smiling at
him so big my face is practically going to bust, and
he's looking at me just the same way, and I figure he
must be thinking exactly the same thing.

I'm dying to know how this all came about, and
why he didn't at least e-mail me first to tell me, but
that phone is still ringing.

Nana Anna goes to answer the phone, and a
minute later I hear her call, "Lacey! It's for you!"

When I get to the phone, she mouths *It's a boy*,
raising her eyebrows at me. I know what she's

thinking. The past few years since Sam moved away I've practically been living a nunlike existence, with only Margot phoning or stopping by, unless it's a prank. Now there's a boy in the entry hall, a boy on the phone—boys are suddenly everywhere!

I take the phone from her, thinking it must be a prank. It's probably Fred Johnson calling up to make some kind of "Lacey Underwire" joke. He likes to do that sometimes when he gets bored, but in the past he's always hung up if Nana Anna answers.

Only it's not Fred Johnson's voice I hear after I say a cautious "Hello?"

"Hi. Lacey?" a deep voice says.

Omigod. It's Chad Wilcox.

"Yes?" I say, trying to look nonchalantly at Nana Anna and Sam, who are watching me through the open doorway. There's nothing between me and Sam, of course—how could there ever be anything between me and Sam?—and yet, somehow, I don't want him to know that it's a boy I like calling me on the phone. "This is she."

"This is Chad Wilcox," he says. "We met at the mall last week."

As if I don't already know. Omigod. *Chad Wilcox!*

"Listen," he goes on, "you're probably wondering how I got your number, since you never gave it to me."

"That's true," I say.

"Every day for the last week, I've gone to the video arcade, looking for you, hoping maybe we could play Lord of the Rings together again."

"That would be nice."

"But when you never showed, I decided to get resourceful. I actually looked in a phone book. Do you know you're the only Underhill in town?"

"Yes," I say, "I did know that."

"So then it was easy to call you and, well, I just did."

"I'm glad."

God, I feel like such a dork. With my short answers, I must sound like I'm not really interested, when I am. I am! But I can't say any more than I'm saying because (1) I'm too freaked out, and (2) Sam and Nana Anna are still standing *right there*.

"So I was wondering," Chad says, clearing his throat—I can just see that manly Adam's apple bobbing—and for the first time sounding unsure, "would you like to maybe go out with me sometime?

I could pick you up and we could go play video games again or maybe go to a movie or . . ."

Now Nana Anna is mouthing *Who IS that?* at me, so I have to speed this up.

"That sounds like it could be good," I say. Then, knowing I can't make a real date in front of Nana Anna, I add, "But I can't commit to, um, an exact time right now. Why don't you give me your number and I'll call you back when we can do that thing?"

And just that simple, he does.

Thank God I'm so good with numbers. I don't even need to scurry around looking for a pencil and paper, which would give Nana Anna more time to get suspicious, because I can memorize it the first time. Memorizing phone numbers is a lot more simple than most people think. It has to do with something called chunking, and it was invented by a guy named Maimonides and . . .

But never mind that now.

Chad Wilcox wants to go out with me!

"Who was that?" Nana Anna asks as soon as I put down the phone.

"Hmm?" I say, distracted. I'm still dreaming about Chad Wilcox.

"That boy," Nana Anna says. "Who was it?"

And now both she and Sam are looking at me funny.

"Oh," I say, coming back down to Earth and trying to think up a good one. Fast. "That was my science lab partner from school. We have to work on a project together. He was trying to set up a time when we could do that. But he's one of those over-eager types who always worries about getting his work done and the project's not due for a while, so I told him I'd call him back."

"But," Nana Anna wants to know, "if he's a Wainscot boy, why did you have to ask for his number? You could have just looked in the school directory. It would be right there."

"Oh, duh." My laugh sounds tinny even to my own ears. I smack myself on the side of the head. "Silly me." Ouch—in an effort to seem devil-may-care I somehow managed to hit myself too hard.

I catch Sam looking at me funny. I know what he's probably thinking: *What kind of idiot hits herself too hard in the side of the head?*

But that's not what he says.

"You've . . . changed," he says.

"What do you mean?"

"You look . . . *different* somehow."

Oh, no. I go into complete internal-panic mode again. Somehow, even with my careful efforts to put on a giant sweatshirt—it even says XXL on the front in big broken letters—he's still noticed how big my breasts have gotten. Shoot! I wanted Sam to think of me as the girl he used to know.

Suddenly he snaps his fingers.

"I know!" he says. "It's your eye!"

"*Excuse* me?" I say. My eye? What's he—

"Your left eye," he cuts me off. "Your right eye looks normal, but it looks like your left eye has black gook all over it."

Oh, brother.

"That's *all* that's changed about me?" He hasn't seen me in three years and the only difference he notices is that I've got gook in my eye? I know it's unreasonable, but I'm miffed. "There's nothing else different?"

He grins widely at the silliness, the unreasonableness that is me.

"I don't know," he says. "It's so hard to say. It's like

84

nothing's changed and everything's changed, all at once. If you know what I mean."

And, somehow, I do.

The next morning, instead of starting on my English essay, which I really had planned to do, I find myself surfing the Web, looking for solutions to having big breasts.

The night before, after I cleaned the mascara gook off my left eye, Sam stayed for dinner, having spaghetti and meatballs with Nana Anna and me.

Having survived Sam showing up out of the blue and Chad calling on the phone, all at once there was one thing I really wanted to know:

"Why didn't you call me first or at least e-mail"— I swatted Sam's shoulder with my dinner napkin— "and tell me your family was moving back?"

Sam thought about it for a minute. "I honestly don't know," he finally said. "I think it was because I kept hoping for so long that my family would move back. But then, every time I thought my dad might get transferred back, it'd all fall apart. I guess I thought it might jinx it somehow if I told anyone else about it." And then Sam did something I don't remember him ever doing before: He blushed. "And I guess I thought it would be amazing just to see the surprised look on your face when you found me on your doorstep."

Then, to celebrate Sam and me being reunited after three years apart, Nana Anna broke out the vanilla ice cream and chocolate syrup.

Before leaving, Sam asked if I wanted to do something the next day, if I still had my baseball mitt.

I do, of course. Playing catch was one of the things Sam and I used to like to do together, although my mitt hasn't gotten any use since he moved away. Catch is really cool because it's easy, you get some exercise in, and you can have great conversations while you're playing.

So I said yes, I'd love to play, but when I got up this morning I realized it was going to be another hot day, and I'm sick of wearing my camouflage clothes all the time. I'd probably sweat to death in this heat if I wore a sweatshirt today. Damn this global warming!

I want to be able to wear a T-shirt, like any normal girl would do on such a hot day. I want to wear my favorite T-shirt, the faded pink one that says SPANKY'S FRANKS on the front. But if I wear it with just my bra underneath, my 36Cs will be too apparent to Sam, and even the sports bra I wear for gym at school, while controlling some of the jiggling, isn't enough to mask these babies.

So that's why I'm sitting here in my room, surfing the Web on my computer, looking for ways to decrease my breast size. I'm not looking for anything like breast-reduction surgery, which is the first solution I turn up, because: (1) it's too drastic, and (2) I have to be ready to play ball in a few hours and there's not enough time.

Then, just when I'm about to give up, I find exactly what I'm looking for:

Geishas.

No, I don't want to become a geisha—there's not enough time for that either; all that training—but I do want to do what geishas do to create that image of an almost boyish figure. They bind their breasts.

I go to the bathroom and look through Nana Anna's medicine cabinet—Nana Anna is very well stocked for any possible medical emergency—until I find exactly what I'm looking for: gauze tape and

Ace bandages, last used the time I sprained my ankle at gymnastics.

I took gymnastics from age three until the summer after fifth grade and was really good at it, but I stopped when middle school started because (1) there was so much more homework in middle school, it interfered with my studies, and (2) my breasts grew too much. But I still like doing back handsprings . . . when no one's looking.

I tape myself using the gauze tape first, finishing it off with the Ace bandages. Then I stand on the toilet and lean out so I can see the total effect in the mirror over the sink.

Not bad. It doesn't make me look as small as I did when I was nine—the last time Sam saw me playing catch—but it definitely reduces the effect of my breasts. Drastically. And, hey, no surgery involved!

But, ouch. Because, you know, it's not all that easy to breathe like this.

Poor geishas.

I sneak back across the hall to my bedroom and grab my pink T-shirt.

Normally, on a nice Saturday like this, Margot and I would be hanging out together. But when I called her this morning to ask if she wanted to join us, she said no, that she really wanted to get started working on that English essay.

It's so unlike Margot. She's always willing to punt schoolwork in favor of fun, whereas I've always been the one who was more concerned about keeping grades up first. It's Nana Anna's training: work before pleasure. But I'm sure Margot's not blowing me off because she wants to work. I'll bet anything she's still mad about the fight we had yesterday over going to the mall, what to do when we got to the mall, and Chad Wilcox in general. (I still can't believe Chad Wilcox called me yesterday!!) This makes me doubly glad that Sam is back. At least now with Margot acting so strange on me, I'll have a buddy to do stuff with.

That English essay. I know I should be working on it, but there's still the rest of the weekend left. I mean, it's only Saturday, and there's too much fun stuff to do today.

I put on the pink T-shirt over my bound breasts and look in the full-length mirror.

Showtime.

. . .

Last night Sam suggested we play catch today at Grayson Park, which would have been really cool, but Nana Anna says now that she's going to be too busy regrouting the tub to drive us, and Sam's mom says she's still too busy unpacking.

So instead he comes over to my place, which isn't bad, since our front yard is plenty big enough to play.

"Wow, Lacey, you look different than you did last night," is the first thing Sam says when he walks over to my yard and finds me waiting for him, mitt in hand.

Inside I'm thinking it's because my breasts are almost flat now, but out loud I say, "That's because I don't have a giant orange sweatshirt on or mascara on one eye anymore." I pound my fist into my mitt. "Let's play ball."

And that's what we do, throwing the ball back and forth, even building up a little sweat as we do it, all the while having one of those great while-playing-catch conversations I mentioned earlier.

Sometimes I think that this is one of the reasons guys have different relationships with one another than girls do. Girls just talk, talk, talk, but guys talk while *doing* stuff. Somehow the friendship comes across even though the path is less obvious.

"What was it like out in Chicago?" I ask.

"Windy," he says with a deep laugh.

It's tough for me to get used to this: Sam now has a deep laugh. In a way, it's like what he said the night before, about everything being the same and everything being different.

"It's very windy out there," he goes on, "and it was really hard for me to make friends at first." He pauses. "I missed you, Lacey."

"Hey, I missed you, too."

Thwack.

"What have you been up to lately?" he asks.

"You mean the last three years?" I laugh. "Let's see. Well, middle school. Middle school has happened since you left and, omigod, it's so much harder than lower school was. In a way, I'm dreading upper school next year, because I can't imagine the work being any harder than it is now, and yet I know it must be. Oh, and I quit gymnastics."

Sam practically drops the ball.

"But you loved gymnastics!" he says, his voice cracking at the end. I guess his voice still does that sometimes when he's excited. "You were so great at it!" His voice cracks again and I see him swallow hard before continuing; it's like he's trying to force his voice back down to its new register. "Why would you ever stop?"

I can't tell him the real reason I gave it up, that I got self-conscious about having the world see me do gymnastics in my new body, because he's not even supposed to know about my new body, so I just shrug, like it doesn't matter, like it was never that important to me in the first place.

"I guess I just outgrew it is all," I say.

"Bummer," he says. "It used to be so much fun to watch you. Hey, can you still do a back handspring?"

"Yep," I say proudly.

Thwack.

"So," Sam tells me, "now that I'm back in town, I'll be going to the public middle school, so we still won't be in the same school."

"Bummer," I say, although inside I'm relieved. It would be great to have my best friend at Wainscot, but if he were at Wainscot, he'd know about all the other guys calling me Lacey Underwire.

"I wonder if anyone will remember me," he says.

"Are you kidding me? Of course they'll remember you. You're Sam Samuels. You're unforgettable!"

Thwack.

Honk!

What was that? That was not the sound of a ball hitting the center of a mitt. That was the sound of someone honking a horn.

I turn to see that a silver VW has pulled up to the curb in front of my house. I squint against the sun to try to make out who's behind the wheel, but before I can, the driver's door opens and up pops the head of . . .

"Chad Wilcox?" I say, surprised.

"Hey," he says, then blushes. He looks so cute when he does that.

I run over to the car, leaving Sam behind me.

"Hey," he says again, "I was just driving by and figured I'd stop and, you know, say hey, see what you were up to."

"But how did you know where I live?"

"When I looked up your number in the phone book, it listed your address, too. So I"—he almost, but not quite, blushes—"you know, figured I'd stop by."

That's so sweet!

Then he looks at me more closely. "Hey, you somehow look . . . *different* from the day I met you."

Oh, no, I think. Of course I look different now— that's because I practically don't have any breasts anymore!

Quickly, to camouflage my lack of breasts, I cross my arms across my chest.

"Must be the strong sunlight today," I stammer. "You know—woo! The sun's in my eyes!"

At some point, I think, I'm going to have to stop acting so dorky around this guy.

From somewhere behind me, I hear Sam clear his throat.

"Look," I say, "this really isn't a very good time. I'm kind of busy right now."

"Right." Chad looks over my shoulder at Sam. "Boyfriend?"

I'm so shocked at the very idea. "God, no!" I say.

Chad squints. Sam is standing on the other side of the lawn, pretty far away from us.

"Little brother?" Chad asks, trying again.

"No," I say. And somehow the idea of being related to Sam is weirder than the idea of him as a boyfriend.

"That's just Sam. We've been neighborhood buddies for, like, forever."

"So," Chad says, obviously relieved, "when do you think you might want to—"

"I've got your number," I interrupt. I can't believe I'm saying this even as I'm saying it. But if I don't get rid of him soon, Nana Anna will probably take a break from regrouting the tub, she'll come out on the porch to chug a Gatorade and fan herself, and then I'll get caught. "I promise, when the time is right, I'll call you."

"I guess that's got to be good enough," says Chad. He smiles and, thankfully, leaves.

"Who was that?" Sam asks, coming over once Chad is gone. "Boyfriend?"

"God, no," I say to deflect him, all the while thinking inside, *But I wish he was.*

We continue playing catch, but I can't stop thinking about what I said to Chad, that I'd call him when the time was right.

MONDAY COMES, AND I'M NOT PREPARED for English class.

How did this happen?

Oh, yeah. That's right. After spending all day playing catch with Sam on Saturday, and having pizza with him and Nana Anna at night, on Sunday Sam and I went to see the new Tom Cruise movie. I knew I should be working on my English essay, but it was my best friend's first weekend back home and there would still be a few hours left after the movie to do schoolwork.

Nana Anna dropped us off and we sat in the theater, munching popcorn and Raisinets, slurping giant sodas, laughing out loud every time there was a scene with Tom running. There were a lot of those, and Sam found them just as funny as I did. Then we bought some more tickets, went across the theater, and sat through the new Brangelina movie. And after that, we finished off the day by watching some Disney flick about an entire family of talking beavers.

I really wanted to kick one of those beavers.

I felt guilty admitting this out loud, but Sam totally got it.

"I'll even hold the little guy for you," he offered.

And I was really stuffed by the end—all that popcorn and candy and soda, the consumption of which made the bindings on my breasts really dig into my skin—but I felt good, too. The last time Sam and I went to a movie together was back in the day when we were not allowed to go see anything rated PG-13, and now we'd seen two of them together and we'd laughed a lot while seeing them. Hell, we'd laughed a lot during the beavers, too. If my breasts hadn't been bound so tightly, I'd have laughed harder.

At one point, hearing Sam's new deep laugh, I turned to look at him. Studying his profile in the darkened theater, I wondered what other girls our age would see looking at him, and I was surprised to realize how cute they'd think he was. And easy to be with. Sam was so easy to be with.

"What?" he said, catching me looking.

"Nothing. I was just thinking about how much fun I'm having."

Then, not five minutes later, it was like the same thing happened, only in reverse. I was laughing at something on the screen when I felt eyes staring at me from the side.

"What?" I said, catching Sam looking.

"Nothing," he said, but I could make out his smile in the dark. "I was just thinking about how much fun I'm having here with you."

Of course, when I got home I was too full of junk food, my head filled with too many celluloid images, to think about anything so mundane as having to write an English essay.

All weekend long I daydreamed about when the opportunity might arise for me to call Chad— I would reach for the phone, wanting to call him, but then I'd realize I didn't really have anything to say and wouldn't, not until I figured out a way for us to see each other again. Meanwhile, I kept telling myself I had to do that English essay. And then I kept telling myself there was still time to get it done. But as time marched on, with the weekend drawing to a close, it became apparent that there simply weren't enough hours left to do the essay properly. And then the exhilarating, slightly crazy, dancing-on-the-edge-of-a-teacup thought occurred to me: *So what if I'm a little late this time? I've always been so perfect, I've always handed everything in on time. What harm can one late essay do?*

And then I went back to daydreaming about when I'd be able to call Chad. Of course he wanted to go out with me, so I would have to wait to call him until I could figure out a way to go out with him, which might not be easy. . . .

Which is why I'm here on Monday, mission unaccomplished.

"Ms. Underhill," Mr. Fitzgerald says when he stops me after class, Mr. Fitzgerald being the kind of teacher who believes in showing kids the same respect he expects, "is there a good reason why your paper isn't ready on time?"

I strain my brain trying to come up with a plausible excuse, but all I can come up with is a wincing "Popcornitis?"

"Are you asking me or telling me?" he says.

Gee, right now he's looking at me so sternly, he doesn't look FitzDreamy at all.

"Celluloid overdose?" I try again.

"It's really not funny, Ms. Underhill. Grades are no laughing matter. In our short time here together at Wainscot I've found you to be one of my more thoughtful students, and I must confess I'm shocked you'd be so lax about an assignment." Being the youngest on staff at twenty-two, it's like Mr. Fitzgerald thinks he has to overcompensate by being more formal, so he talks much older but only winds up sounding like a stuffy old geezer. Now he lowers the boom. "I'm disappointed in you."

Ooh, that's a low blow! I think all adults, everywhere, know intuitively that the worst thing you can say to a certain kind of kid—a kid like me—is that you're "disappointed" in us.

"I'm sorry," I tell him. "I'll do better. I promise I'll get it done."

"Of course you'll get it done." He looks at his watch as though it's a calendar. "You have until Thursday."

"That's fair." I start to leave.

"And Ms. Underhill," he says, stopping me, "if I were you, I'd make sure it's an A paper. That way, at least you'll still wind up with a B."

"A B?" I don't understand. I always get As in English. I get As in almost everything I do.

"Yes," he says, "a B. Since you don't have any good excuse for why you didn't hand your paper in on time, it wouldn't be fair to the other students for me to grade you in the same way, now, would it?"

"I guess—"

"So I'll be docking you a full grade off whatever your true grade is. Dismissed."

Ooh . . . *harsh.*

So I spend that day after school and Tuesday and Wednesday working on my paper, turning it in on Thursday.

"I look forward to reading this," is all Mr. Fitzgerald says as he tucks it into his briefcase.

At least now I have the opportunity to get a B.

Thursday after school has always been one of Margot's and my unofficial times for definitely doing something together, even if that something is only homework. Margot has an older sister in college who says Thursday nights are the biggest nights on campus for partying, because so many kids go home for the weekends. Pretending Thursday is our party night too always makes us feel older than we are.

But when I ask Margot what she wants to do after school, she says she can't do anything with me this week.

At least it's for a good reason.

"Wonder of wonders," she whispers so no one else will hear her as we talk next to our lockers, "Liam SchwartzDreamy is my science partner, and we're going to be working on a project after school today. At his place. It'll probably take several hours."

"Bonus!" I say, happy for her. "This could be your big chance with him!"

"Ya think?" She makes a wry face. "Well, I don't. I think he likes someone else."

"Who?"

"You."

"No way!"

"Yes, way. You are, after all, Lacey Underwire, aren't you?"

And she walks away.

I'm left standing there, thinking my friend is nuts, when a positive thought occurs to me:

This is my big chance.

As soon as I get home, I call the number Chad gave me, my stomach doing somersaults all the while. It turns out to be his cell and he answers right away, the sound of bells and whistles loud in the background; he must be at the video arcade at the mall.

After me saying, "Well, I'm finally calling" and him saying, "I'm so glad you did," I get straight down to business.

"I'm free this evening," I tell him, correcting to, "well, this afternoon. Sometime between this evening and afternoon. Do you still want to do something?"

He does, and he suggests a movie, but when he talks about picking me up, things get tricky. I can't have him picking me up at my house, because if Nana Anna sees a sixteen-year-old pick me up to go out on a date she'll never let me out of the house. But I don't drive yet, so I can't drive myself to meet him, and I certainly can't have Nana Anna drop me off.

"I already know where you live," he says when I

tell him I need to give him the address where to pick me up.

"Yes, but you can't pick me up there," I say.

"I can't?"

"No, because I won't be there." I think fast. "I'll be studying first at my friend Margot's house. You remember Margot? You met her with me that day at the mall?" I keep talking fast, so he can't say anything, giving him Margot's address. *This will work*, I think. *I can tell Nana Anna I'll be studying at Margot's, then I can walk around the corner to Margot's, since Margot won't be there anyway, and wait for Chad to arrive.*

Phew! I'm exhausting myself!

"Oh," I add, winding down, "and I won't be able to stay out too late." I wince even as I say it, knowing how lame I must sound to Chad's sixteen-year-old ears. "It's just that my grandmother, who I live with, has this thing about not being out too late on school nights."

"No problem," Chad says. "I promise to have you home before you turn into a pumpkin."

I laugh nervously. "Actually, the pumpkin hour would be too late. It'll have to be more like ten."

"No problem," he says again, his laugh easy. "I'll bring you home whenever you want."

Then he arranges to pick me up at four forty-five, which must seem to him like an insanely early hour to start a date but which falls in line with the lies I plan to tell Nana Anna.

I hang up the phone and then it hits me:

I'm going on a date—my first date!

Omigod, I'm going on my first date . . . and I have no idea what to wear!

I immediately reject the gauze top I rejected when I tried it on the week before. It's just too mature. I don't think I'll ever be as mature as that top. Then I consider the crimson satin number, but I reject that, too: it shows too much cleavage and is way too dressy for a first date at the movies . . . not that I really know what I'm talking about here.

At last I settle on my pink SPANKY'S FRANKS T-shirt. It's tight enough that when I wear it without the breast-binding material underneath, it makes my body look sixteen. And since we're just going to the movies, this should work.

So that's what I'm wearing when I'm standing in

Margot's driveway, waiting, and I see Chad pull up in his car.

He gets out to open my door for me—such good manners!—and I'm all the while hoping no one in Margot's family looks out the window right now and sees what I'm doing.

Thankfully, the blinds stay closed and I see no draperies moving.

"Wow," Chad says as I sit down in the passenger's seat, swinging in my jeans-clad legs, "you must really love that shirt."

"Excuse me?"

"Isn't that the same shirt you were wearing when I saw you playing catch the other day?"

Well, of course it is. And if Chad weren't standing right there, I'd hit myself in the head for doing such a "duh" thing.

"What's the matter?" I say, trying for coy but probably sounding defensive. "You don't like it?"

"Oh, no," he says quickly. "It looks great on you, but, um, it does look different for some reason than it did the other day. And yet I can't exactly figure out why. . . ."

Well, of course it looks different, I want to tell him.

The other day I didn't have breasts . . . and now I do!

"Anyway," he says, "you look great. You make that T-shirt look great."

Swoon!

. . .

On the way to the theater, Chad makes small talk about school.

He says his is okay and asks me how I like mine.

"It's okay," I say, not wanting to sound like a private-school brat. "It's, you know, a school."

"I never went to a private school," he says, "but I sort of know some guys who went to Wainscot. Do you know Brad Dylan and Jason Bono?" He's just named two guys who graduated the year before.

Out loud I say, "Well, I know who they are," while inside I'm thinking, *but I'm sure they don't know who I am.*

"That's cool," he says. "They're not really close friends anyway, you know? I was just wondering."

I watch as he steers the car. I never realized before what a masculine thing driving a car can be, but he does it so masculinely, I could watch him do it all night. And it's nice to just watch him and not talk. Talking somehow feels awkward, strained, not at all like it did when Sam and I went to the movies. It's like we're looking for things to say to each other. But watching him? That I could do all day and all night.

Eventually we get to the movie theater, and I realize there are only three movies that are starting anytime soon: the Tom Cruise movie, the Brangelina movie, and the one with the beavers.

There's no way I want to see those damn beavers again—Chad gives me a strange look when I ask him if he'd hold a beaver for me while I kicked it—or the Brangelina, so I suggest the Tom Cruise, failing to mention that I've already seen it with Sam. I don't want to mention Sam, because that'll give Chad reason to ask again if Sam's my boyfriend or something.

When it's time to pay for our tickets, I start to reach into my handbag to pay for mine, but Chad stops me.

"No way," he says. "I've got you covered. I'm taking you out, even if it was technically you who called me."

And it's the same at the concession stand.

So that's how I find myself in a movie theater, for the second time within a week watching Tom Cruise run for his life repeatedly to escape bad guys. But it's weird because whenever Tom starts running, I start laughing, then I look over to see if Chad is laughing, but he's not laughing with me, not like Sam did.

Then I stop to realize that I, Lacey Underhill, am sitting here in the dark with a boy at the movie theater! A boy who's not Sam!

It feels so, I don't know, like nothing I've ever done before. It's like I can smell him in the dark, over and above the smell of popcorn; like I can feel him next to me, even though no parts of our bodies are making contact. Every one of my senses feels alive with the presence of *him*, the nearness, and I really feel it when he casually puts his arm around my shoulders.

It's such a surprise, though, feeling his arm around me, that I give a little jump. So then he takes my hand in his instead and I jump a little at that, too, but he holds on tight.

It's like I'm two people at once: me, Lacey Underhill, the girl Nana Anna and Sam and Margot and everyone at Wainscot knows, while at the same time I'm Lacey, this girl who's sitting in a darkened movie theater having her hand held by an incredibly cute guy while Tom Cruise races across the screen for his life.

But then, when the movie is nearly over, Chad

leans closer to whisper in my ear, asking me where I want to go next, and all of a sudden the good feelings that have been flaming inside of me turn to ash. I can't help it. All I can think about are the lies I told Nana Anna to get myself here. Here is where I want to be more than anything, next to Chad, but the guilt won't let me stay.

"I know this is lame," I whisper back, "but could you take me home afterward? My grandmother hasn't been feeling too good lately and, well, I don't like to leave her alone for too long."

So we watch Tom Cruise run his way back to safety and a happy ending that I'm seeing for the second time, and then Chad drives me home, back to my house this time, not Margot's driveway.

All the while, he's silent and I wonder if he's mad at me for cutting our date short.

When we get to my house, he says he'll walk me to my door, but I can't have that. What if Nana Anna sees him there?

So instead I say, "Um, that's okay. We can say good-bye here."

"Is it okay if I kiss you before you go?" he asks shyly.

Oh, *man*! What do I say to *that*?

"Of course," I say, trying to sound cool, as if guys ask me this all the time.

And then his lips softly brush against mine and—omi*god*—this is my first kiss!

His lips are warm and sweet, maybe from the soda, and a little salty, too, maybe from the popcorn.

I like this kiss. It's good, and I realize that as much as I've been looking forward to this inside my head—my first kiss!—I was somehow scared of it too. I guess I was thinking that if I kissed Chad, or any boy, it would be like saying yes to a whole lot else. But this is sweet and wonderful. It's just its own thing—a kiss—and it feels just right.

"I really like you, Lacey," he says, breaking the lip-lock. "I like everything about you. I like the way you play pinball, I like the way you laugh in the movies, I like the way you worry about your grandmother."

He likes all that about *me*? Even the last part? And here I thought I'd blown it, but it turns out I haven't blown it at all!

"I hope you like me, too," he adds.

All I can do is nod dumbly, numbly.

"So," he says, "can we do this again?"

I pucker up, move in for another kiss.

He laughs. "I didn't mean that, although I do want to do that again. But I meant go out—will you go out with me again?"

I'm stumped, thinking of the logistics of going out with him again. Tonight it worked out, but only because Margot bailed on me and I told all those lies to Nana Anna. But I can't go on counting on fate to drop opportunities in my lap.

"That's okay," he says, perhaps seeing how stumped I am. "Tell you what: How about we leave it that the next time you want to go out with me, you give me a call again?"

And in the dark of the car, with the moonlight streaming in, I can see that somehow, mercifully, he's not offended by this setup at all.

And then he kisses me one more time.

Only this time it's a different sort of kiss. The way he kisses me now is deeper, as though somehow the very kiss itself is probing for something more, pushing for something bigger. He's still Chad, and I'm still Lacey, but somehow this kiss is scaring me on some level and I'm actually relieved to get out of the car.

9.

THE NEXT DAY, FRIDAY, I MAKE AN
executive decision to change my look, at least at
school. I will no longer be "Lacey, Who Wears Sweater-
Vests and Blazers in Ninety-Degree Weather." (The
September heat wave is still going strong.) I will be
like everyone else. I will be normal, finally.

I feel the confidence to do this now because I have
Chad in my corner, Chad who wants to see me again
even though I act so downright weird around him. If
I can attract the attention of an older boy, what do I
have to fear anymore about the childish reactions to
my body from thirteen- and fourteen-year-olds?

So, rather than dressing like I'm going to the
North Pole, I simply put on my white button-down
blouse over my plaid skirt, the tails hanging out,

tossing the sleeved version of the navy school sweater nonchalantly around my shoulders, letting the sleeves hang down in front oh-so-casually, as though I have complete confidence that no untied sweater would ever dare fall off *my* shoulders.

"That's a good look for you," Nana Anna says when I come down for breakfast.

This gives me a moment's pause. I love Nana Anna, but what does it say about my new look, that my pea-soup-loving grandmother who favors polyester as if there is no other fabric in the world thinks it's good?

I munch my way through a stack of French toast, and when I get on the bus, John Fredericks and Fred Johnson are there to greet me as usual.

"Morning, Lacey," John says, choosing the high road.

"Lacey Underwire," says Fred, taking the low road, "this is so cool—I can finally see your underwires!"

But for once, I am not bothered by him.

"In your dreams, middle-school boy," I say, brushing past.

When I walk into school, Margot is standing by our lockers. I'm sure she wants to tell me about her night with Liam. I know I want to tell her about my night with Chad. Even though Margot hasn't been supportive in the past of my liking of Chad, I'm sure that once she hears what a gentleman he was last night she will change her tune. Of course, I won't tell her how his last kiss kind of made me feel uncomfortable. In fact, I don't really let myself think much now about that second kiss either. I focus instead on the first kiss, the perfect kiss.

"So?" I say, seeing the big grin on her face. "*Spill.*" And she does.

"Omigod, Lacey, you would not believe how cool it was! Here I was thinking Liam secretly liked you, because, you know, all the guys are always staring at you all the time, but I'm really starting to think maybe he likes me instead."

"That's great!" I say, meaning it. "And of course he likes you. Who wouldn't? But, tell me, what was your first clue?"

"Well, actually, there were two clues," she says conspiratorially. "First, when I got to his house, he told me he was glad we were science partners, because he thinks I'm really good at science."

I try to muster up some enthusiasm for this. "Hey,

that's a great start, but what was the second clue?"

"Well, when I left," she says, "he said that he was right and I *was* really good at science."

I confess, this does not exactly seem like the opening scenes from *Romeo and Juliet*, but it's good to see Margot look so excited about something, particularly something to do with a boy. It's also good because it gives me my own opening. I've had my first real kiss. I'm dying to tell her about it! I mean, if I don't tell Margot, who can I tell?

"That's awesome news," I say, "and the timing couldn't be better because I have some awesome news too."

Then I proceed to tell her, in one breathless loop, about my night with Chad. It's not until I'm nearly done that I notice the smile has slid right off her face. When I stop talking she says, "I don't think this is awesome at all! In fact, I think it's the worst thing you've ever done."

"What are you talking about?"

Okay, so maybe I shouldn't have been expecting her to jump straight across the aisle from being skeptical about Chad to totally loving the idea of him, but *this*?

"You *lied* to Nana Anna," she points out, as if this is something I don't already know.

"Yes, but—"

"Lying to Nana Anna has to be worse than breaking, like, nearly all of the Ten Commandments at once."

"Actually, one of the commandments is about not lying, only it doesn't refer to Nana Anna specifically. I'm pretty sure it's just supposed to be a more general commandment."

"*And*," she goes on as if I haven't even spoken, ignoring, I must point out, my clever use of sarcasm, "you used *me* as part of your lies. Look, if you want to screw up your life by continuing to see Chad, that's your business. But I absolutely *forbid* you to use my driveway as a means of doing so. Next time you want to lie to Nana Anna, think of somewhere else to have Chad pick you up."

And she stalks off.

Miraculously, she doesn't stay mad at me the whole day.

When lunch comes, we sit together like we usually do, and I break the silence after Deanna and Patty say something about the string beans on Margot's plate being a perfect metaphor for the shape of her body. I counter by pointing out that the peas on their plates— at least one veg at lunch is obligatory at Wainscot—is the perfect metaphor for their tiny little minds.

"And," I add, "while it is likely that Margot's shape will one day change, perhaps turning into a cauliflower, it is highly unlikely that your low IQs ever will. You, I'm afraid, will always be peas."

There is nothing better for bringing two girls close together again than successfully putting down two other girls who were being mean first.

But then it is time for gym class and the fun ends.

I think it's crazy this year that we have gym right after lunch. Didn't anyone in this school ever hear about the need to rest after eating? If I lived in Europe, my life would be so much better right now because then I would be on a siesta after my fiesta. And while I was on my siesta, I could try to come up with a plan for seeing Chad again so I could call him, like, *right this minute*.

All that running around after the pukey lunches they give us in the cafeteria always makes me, well, want to puke. And it is particularly hard now because not only are we running, but we are doing way too much jumping, this being volleyball week.

I hate volleyball week. I hate it that our gym class is coed. I hate having coed classes during volleyball week because Ms. Tank, the teacher, will no longer allow me to wear my navy sweatshirt over my white T-shirt and navy shorts, because she says she is worried I will pass out in the gym that has no air-conditioning. I hate having coed classes during volleyball week because every time I jump to hit the ball, making my breasts jiggle under my white T-shirt, Fred Johnson snorts.

I have a lot of hatred going on in me right now. I am beginning to think this might not be good for my soul.

So, in order to make myself start hating less, I stop jumping when the ball comes my way, so my breasts won't jiggle. This means, however, that, being short, I can't get the ball over the net, and Ms. Tank yells at me.

"What's wrong, Underhill? Do you have cement in your sneakers?"

"No," Fred snickers, speaking just low enough so Ms. Tank (who is somewhat deaf, which is why she yells so much) can't hear him, "but she's got something in her sports bra."

"Shut. Up." That's how I respond. It's so funny. I used to be kind of intimidated by people making fun of me and Margot, but now I'm telling people off right and left.

I'm actually thinking about telling Fred off some more, when the school secretary comes down the stairs to the gym and hands a note to Ms. Tank.

"Underhill?" Ms. Tank yells a minute later. "You need to go to the office. Mr. Powers wants to see you . . . *now*!"

Crap. What did I do wrong? Can they really be thinking of expelling me already just because I handed one measly English paper in late?

But when I get to Mr. Powers's office, I learn the real reason I've been called there.

The headmaster is sitting behind his desk, wearing his red power tie, his tiny diamond earring firmly in place. I think Mr. Powers thinks wearing an earring rather than a tie clip makes him look cool and that the school board thinks having a headmaster with an earring is cool. Me, I just hope I'm not about to get in trouble for anything too big.

In one of the visitor chairs in the office sits Ms.

Blackwell, her whistle on a chain around her neck. She and I have had no reason to talk in the past, but I know she's the girls' athletic director for the upper school, the upper school here being what high school would be anywhere else.

"Please sit, Ms. Underhill," Mr. Powers says, indicating the other visitor chair.

As I sit, I notice some peculiar items on his desk: a navy blue pleated miniskirt and matching top, a pair of pom-poms. It's the uniform of the Wainscot cheerleading squad.

"Um," I say, "this isn't about my English paper, is it?"

"English paper?" Mr. Powers looks confused. "No, of course not. It's about something else. Ms. Blackwell?"

"Lacey," Ms. Blackwell starts, "I don't know if you heard, and being in the middle school you probably didn't, but Tara Trump broke her leg yesterday. She was hanging upside down in a tree and fell out of it. To keep from landing on her head, she did a twist midair but wound up landing—ungracefully, I might add—on her own leg."

"Oh, no," I say, "that's awful."

"It is," Ms. Blackwell agrees. "It's a real tragedy,

because now the Wainscot cheerleading squad has only five cheerleaders. That's an awkward number for a squad. You can't even make a decent pyramid with five cheerleaders. There's no one to go on top!"

"That does sound tragic," I say, even though inside I'm thinking, *But isn't it more tragic for Tara than it is for Ms. Blackwell? And*, I might add, *why are they telling me all this?*

"You're probably wondering why we're telling you all this," says Mr. Powers.

I nod.

"Well," he goes on, "Wainscot needs you right now. We'd like you to consider being the sixth cheerleader."

"*What?*" I say.

"You know," Ms. Blackwell says, as though I haven't interjected so vehemently, "so we can at least still field a decent pyramid."

I'm speechless, and while I'm being speechless, it's a good time to stop rolling the tape so I can explain something here.

Wainscot is small.

"How small is it?" you may well ask, as though this were some kind of bad comedy routine.

Wainscot is so small that everyone in the upper school is required to register for at least one sports team. This means that with Tara Trump breaking her leg, and with every other girl in the upper school already enrolled for the semester in soccer or lacrosse or ultimate Frisbee, there really is nothing else for Ms. Blackwell to do except think outside the box.

That's me now, I'm beginning to suspect: outside the box.

And now we may resume our story.

"Ms. Blackwell and I went over the transcripts of all the eighth-grade girls here at Wainscot," Mr. Powers informs me, "and we saw where you won some awards for gymnastics when you were younger. We agreed that you'd make a fine cheerleader. The question is: Will you do it?"

"You mean I have a choice?" I say.

"Of course," he says. "Upper-school students are required to participate in a sport, but there are no similar rules for middle-school students, so we can't make you do this if you don't want to."

"But it sure would be great," Ms. Blackwell puts in, licking her lips, "if we could make that pyramid."

I have the feeling that before this is done, I will

get sick of hearing about that damn pyramid.

"What exactly would this involve?" I ask, figuring I should at least hear them out.

"Well, you'd need to attend practice every day after school, of course," Ms. Blackwell explains, "and you'd need to cheer at all the scheduled boys' soccer games. The lacrosse and ultimate Frisbee teams, as well as all the girls' teams, are on their own."

How sexist.

This is not what I need in my life. I originally gave up gymnastics because I no longer wanted to expose my leotard-clad body to the sneers of public scrutiny. Why go back there?

But then, just as I'm on the verge of saying no, an intriguing thought enters my brain, my brain being *not* the size of a pea: I've wanted Chad Wilcox to go on perceiving me as being older than I am. What better way to achieve this than to join the cheerleading squad and then invite him to games? It will set in concrete his image of me as being older, since all the cheerleaders are high-school age. So instead of saying no, I open my mouth and say:

"Yes."

10.

AND SO, MY POM-POM DAYS BEGIN.

But not without a few hitches.

When I get home from school, cheerleading uniform and pom-poms in hand, exempt from practice for the first day because I explained to Ms. Blackwell that I haven't arranged for new after-school transportation yet, Nana Anna greets me with, "What are those two things you're holding?" followed by, "Sam was here already. I told him I'd have you go over as soon as you got home. I think he got a new video game."

You'd think that after years apart, and with us both growing up some in between, it would take a while for Sam and me to slip into a new groove together. And yet it hasn't. When we're together, it's like no time has passed at all. Never mind a new groove, we're still in our old groove.

I explain to Nana Anna about the cheerleading squad and how the head cheerleader, Kimmie Parker, will be driving me home after practices and games starting next week. "And," I add, "if Sam does come by on days when I'm not here, please don't tell him I'm doing cheerleading."

"But why not?" Nana Anna wants to know. "Are you ashamed?"

"It's not exactly that," I say, squirming. "I just, I don't know, I just don't want him to know, okay?"

"Well, I'm not going to *lie*," she says, which right away makes me feel guilty again over the lies I told the night I went out with Chad, "so I'll just say you're not here, and I'll say it in an arms-crossed way"— and here she demonstrates—"that invites no further questions. What you tell Sam, on the other hand, that's your own business."

So when I go over to Sam's house, after first running up to my room and binding my breasts, I tell him that I've signed up for programs in cooking and ceramics that'll keep me busy after school, but that whenever I have free time we'll still hang out together.

"Why cooking and ceramics?" asks Sam.

"I'm worried it's been too much for Nana Anna all these years, doing all the cooking. I want to take over some of that responsibility from her, but I want it to be a surprise."

"And the ceramics?"

"Um"—*think fast, Lacey!*—"I want to make a few really cool bowls to put the food I'll be making Nana Anna in."

Then we play Sam's new video game.

On Monday, after another weekend hanging out with Sam—I can't believe how much fun we have together, I can't believe how easy he is to be around; it's like when we're together I even forget to angst about Chad—I return to school, cheerleading gear safely stowed in my backpack. After school, I stay for practice, meeting with the others on the sidelines of the soccer field, where we're to practice as the guys practice their game. I'm nervous at first. I barely even know who these girls are, they're so much older. In addition to Kimmie Parker, there's Sylvia Plant, Heather DeBeer, Missy Taylor, and Amanda Claudel. I can't say they're overly friendly to me, nor are they unfriendly, not like Patty and Deanna always are. It's more like they're grateful to have me be a warm body to fill out the squad and that's it.

But as they teach me routines, and I start getting the hang of things, something shifts inside me and the nerves disappear. It feels great, moving my body like this. For the first time in what seems like forever, I'm not worrying about what anyone who might be looking at me is thinking or seeing. I'm not even worried about all the older guys out on the field seeing me bounce around like this. I'm just enjoying my body for all it can do.

"Not bad," Kimmie says, tossing me a Gatorade when practice is through.

"Thanks," I say, using the bottle to wipe the perspiration from my brow.

"So," she says, "you think you'll be ready in time for the first game of the season Thursday?"

"Are you kidding?" says Ms. Blackwell, coming up to us. "Lacey here is going to be the top of the pyramid."

I get through the next few days of practice and when Thursday—game day—comes, several things happen.

First, I wear my cheerleading uniform to Wainscot for the first time. It's a school thing. On game days, everyone involved—athletes and those who cheer athletes—wear their uniforms. Now that I'm on the squad, this includes me. But me being a uniformed cheerleader, with the short skirt and tight top, elicits a few reactions.

"I can't believe you didn't tell me this!" Margot says when she sees me.

"I'm sorry," I tell her. "I just, I don't know, there wasn't really time. Everything happened so fast. And then you've been so busy studying with Liam lately. Not that there's anything wrong with that," I'm quick to add.

"But we have lunch together every day!" she points out.

"I'm sorry," I say again, lamely, "I guess I just kept forgetting about it."

What I don't say out loud is that maybe I kept "forgetting" because we don't communicate the way we used to. Or maybe I kept "forgetting" because deep down I knew her reaction would be somehow negative.

The next thing that happens is Fred Johnson sees

me. "Who's the new girl?" he quips. "Is this Lacey Pom-Poms I see?"

And that's who I become, right in that moment: Lacey Pom-Poms.

But the worst nickname ever is mitigated by what happens next. Kimmie Parker, Sylvia Plant, Heather DeBeer, Missy Taylor, and Amanda Claudel come striding into the middle-school locker area, which is, like, unheard of. No upper schoolers come back to middle school once they're out, not unless Mr. Powers makes them come do a presentation or something. But here are five seniors, right now, and they come straight up to me.

"Hey," Kimmie says, putting her fist out to bump fists with mine. If I knew what I was doing, I'd already have my hand formed into a fist, which is the universal symbol of solidarity everywhere. But of course I don't know what I'm doing, so my hand is just kind of hanging, attached to my arm at my side, and Kimmie's fist only barely manages to graze my wrist.

"We just wanted to come down to wish you a good game this afternoon," she goes on. "Everyone is rooting for you to hit a home run."

I like Kimmie a lot, especially since we've gotten to know each other better with her being the one who drives me home now at the end of the day, but I have to say, sometimes she doesn't seem to have a firm grasp of what sport we're playing.

"Yeah," adds Heather, "we think it's awesome that, like, you're small enough to fit at the top of the pyramid. When we do it, I always feel like we're pins set up for bowling, only there are six of us instead of ten and we're on our knees instead of standing straight up."

"Um . . . *yeah*," I say. Sometimes I wonder if any of these cheerleading girls are going to the same school I am. And yet I know they're all on the honor roll, so I figure the way they act when they're in their cheerleading uniforms is, well, some sort of act.

"So, like Kimmie says," Sylvia puts in, "have a good game." Sylvia lacks in originality.

"Yeah, score a touchdown," Amanda says. She spends lots of time with Kimmie and Heather.

"Yay, Bulldogs!" cries Missy, one pom-pom on her hip as she raises her other straight in the air. Missy's enthusiasm makes up for all the rest.

Then they turn as a group, their short skirts

twitching behind them as they strut away.

"*Man*," I hear Deanna say to Patty. They've been watching all of this. "Did you see *that*?" They're clearly impressed.

It's like I have instant cool. Even Fred's taunts of "Lacey Pom-Poms" can't stop me now.

"Oh, no," Margot says, horror entering her eyes. "It's like you've gone over to . . . *The Other Side*!"

Despite the mixed reactions of Deanna and Patty (for the first time, they pay attention to me in a not-nasty way at lunch), Margot (she sort of snubs me), and Fred ("Look, guys, it's Lacey Pom-Poms!"—which, let me tell you, I cannot hear enough . . . *not*), my day goes smoothly. That same physical confidence I felt at my first cheerleading practice? It's back again. I used to worry about being special, since that meant I was "different," and the kind of different I was made me not "normal." But it's like all that has disappeared now. It's like I'm *embracing* my difference, maybe even flaunting it a bit. And it's good when I remember what Sam said about how much he used to like seeing me do gymnastics. It makes me feel safe somehow, and I wish he could see me now, but of course he can't, because then he would know I have become Breasts "R" Us.

And I start noticing things changing around me. True, Fred is still a jerk, but when I go to leave the lunchroom, John Fredericks rushes ahead to hold the door for me, and when I slip by him through the gap, he doesn't even say anything rude. He looks like it's his privilege to hold the door for me!

But then English class comes and—how did this happen?—somehow I neglected to write another essay I was supposed to hand in.

Oh, yeah, now I remember how this happened. I spend all my free time thinking about Chad, about how to hide my breasts from Sam and enhance them for Chad. Then, having missed the deadline on one paper, I guess one bad slide led to another.

"Ms. Underhill?" Mr. Fitzgerald says. "See me after class."

Uh-oh.

So after class, as instructed, I see him, because what else can I do? I stand before him, contrite, notebook clasped in my hands behind my back, nervously hitting myself in the butt with it.

"So"—I shuffle my feet—"I suppose the popcorni-tis thing won't work a second time."

Mr. Fitzgerald doesn't say anything for the longest time. The stretched-out silence eventually forces me to look up, like a yo-yo snapped back up to the yo-yo user's hand. If that makes any sense. I think I may have been spending too much time with the Wainscot cheerleading squad lately.

And then . . . omi*god*! Is Mr. Fitzgerald checking out my *breasts*?

He reddens when he sees me catching him and quickly darts his eyes away. Then he relaxes, visibly forcing himself to do so, as if his body is saying, "Nope, nothing to see here, folks, just move along."

Aloud, he says, "Of course the popcornitis alibi won't work again. It didn't work the first time."

Then a weird thing happens, even weirder than catching Mr. Fitzgerald checking out my breasts. Up until now, he's been standing like he always does, leaning against the front of his desk, in this instance with me standing right in front of him. But now he deliberately walks around to the other side of the desk. It's very odd coming from a teacher who prides himself on his ability to build intimacy with his students, even if during those moments of intimacy he still uses that overly formal way of talking. But now it's almost like he wants to—*has* to—put physical distance between us.

It's tough for me to understand what this all means, so I return to the matter at hand.

"So if I hand the paper in late, like last time, and I write an A paper, you'll give me a B?"

"No," he says.

"Oh," I say, dropping my eyes. "So I guess you'll drop me two grades this time, for a second offense, giving me a C."

"That would be cruel and unusual of me," he says, coughing a nervous cough, "not to mention excessive. I can see you'd be a tougher teacher than I am. No, if you hand in your paper on Monday, and it's an A paper, I'll still give you an A."

"You will?" My yo-yo head snaps up again. "But why?"

"Because I . . ." He pauses. He suddenly looks really uncomfortable, and I get the strangest feeling, like he suddenly can't wait to get me out of there. "Because," he goes on in a rush, "I understand you've had a lot thrust upon your shoulders, what with the school calling upon you to . . . fill out the cheerleading squad and all. So"—he shrugs—"I'm giving you a break. Call me the nicest teacher you've ever had, if you like."

I don't know what to call him, since I've never had a teacher check out my breasts before.

I quickly move my notebook to the front, holding it to my chest to protect those breasts, duck my head, thank him, and rush out.

Once in the hallway, the door closed behind me, I'm not sure what I feel.

Why did Mr. Fitzgerald just give me this break? Was it really because of what he said, that I have so much on my plate? It's all so strange, and nothing like the way things have been between Mr. Fitzgerald and me before. Did I really make him feel that uncomfortable? Maybe he originally was going to dock my grade, like he did last time, but then he got so flustered he gave me a break instead?

Ah, who knows what's really going on in other people's heads when they look at me? It's all so confusing. Maybe it's all in my head?

On the one hand, I'm relieved to get the extension on my paper and I can't believe it was as easy as being on the cheerleading squad and wearing my uniform to school today—it *can't* be *just* that. On the other hand, I'm totally skeeved out. Mr. Fitzgerald is cute and everything, for a teacher. I mean, that's why he's FitzDreamy. But he *is* a teacher and much older than me, and even if I only caught him checking me out for just a second . . . *ick*. Still, on the third hand, I may still get an A and . . .

Man, these breasts are powerful!

But I can't think about that right now because I have to focus on the fact that the first game is today and that I've invited Chad to come see me cheer.

11.

CHEERLEADING FOR THE WAINSCOT BOYS'
soccer team is like a dream.

Instead of feeling like an outsider, like I do in my own eighth-grade class, I feel like an *insider* here. The other girls are really grateful to have me, the pyramid with me on top comes off like a charm, and even the boys from the team are kind of friendly to me during halftime. I figure it's because they're in a good mood since they're winning.

Margot has stayed after school to watch me cheer, which makes me feel good, but that good feeling stops when I see her glaring at Chad, who is also there.

But then I forget about Margot completely whenever I look over at Chad and see him grinning at me.

The only thing missing right now is Sam. Sam being here would make everything complete. Not that I'd want him to see me in my cheerleading uniform— I definitely don't want that—but it would be great to have him here for my moment of triumph, to see that I really *can* still nail a back handspring.

It's a complex world sometimes, and it's all mine.

After the game, Margot gets to me first, asking if I want her and her mom to give me a ride home.

I say no, that Kimmie is driving me.

Then Chad comes up.

"You were really great out there!" he says enthusiastically.

"Thanks," I say, pleased with his enthusiasm and also relieved that, having met me as the kind of girl who is good at video games, he doesn't mind that I'm turning out to be the kind of girl who also jumps around with pom-poms in her hands.

"So," he says, "can I give you a lift home?"

I feel the eyes of the entire squad upon me. I *so* want to say yes to him. But I also feel Margot's eyes glaring at both of us, and having just said no to her offer of a ride, how can I now say yes to him? Plus, it's still daylight out. If Nana Anna saw him drop me off, there'd be hell to pay, and if I asked him to drop me off down the street, well, that'd be too weird. Plus, I remember that kiss in the car when he dropped me off after the movies: not the first kiss, the one that was sweet and wonderful, but the one that came afterward. In a way, it makes me feel scared to be in his car again.

"Maybe another time?" I say, hoping my smile looks encouraging. "I'm already riding with Kimmie."

"Is it okay if I give you a kiss before you go, then?" he asks.

I can't believe this is happening. I can't believe I'm about to engage in my first PDA. But how can I say no to Chad?

For an answer—rather than speaking, because I know if I try to say anything right now I'll come off as a geek—I tilt my head toward him. I'm half expecting a peck on the cheek, but he gives it to me full on the lips. At first I'm embarrassed, but then I lose myself in how good it feels. This is like that very first time he kissed me, all over again.

Kissing: what a great invention. I'm thinking I could do this forever.

And I'm still thinking that, and doing it, when I hear the sound of someone coughing. Loudly.

Margot, of course.

Immediately, yet reluctantly, I break the lip-lock.

"I really have to go," I tell Chad.

"No worries," he says with an easy smile. "You'll call me soon, right?"

"Definitely."

In Kimmie's car, on the way home, all she can talk about is Chad.

"That's so cool, Lacey! For one thing, he's gorgeous. And for another thing, I can't believe you're going out with such a cool guy."

Are Chad and I "going out"?

"No offense," she says, "but when I was in eighth grade, whatever else I may have been doing, I was *not* going out with a gorgeous guy old enough to own his own car. No offense," she says again.

"No problem," I tell her. And I'm not offended. If anyone knows how unlikely this all is, it's me. After all, I'm living it. But I love the way Kimmie is looking at me now, the way I know the others must have been looking at me when Chad kissed me after the game:

It's like they've just realized there's more to me than meets the eye.

Kimmie drops me off in the driveway, tooting her horn as she drives away afterward. I give a friendly wave to the retreating taillights and open the front door, pleased with how the day has gone.

"Nana Anna!" I call, dropping my pom-poms and backpack in the entryway. "I'm home!"

No answer.

"Nana Anna?" I call again, moving into the house. I can't wait to tell her how well the game went.

Then I sniff the air and my nose notices something odd: no smells.

"Nana Anna?" I call again, worried now, starting to look for that which should be there because it's always there: Nana Anna.

I find her, at last, on one of the sofas in the living room.

She's lying down. Which makes no sense. Nana Anna never lies down in the daytime. She's always moving, moving, cooking something, painting something, washing windows, regrouting the tub, uprooting a tree.

"Nana Anna?" I say tentatively.

"Lacey," she says, trying to force a smile.

Then I notice she's trembling like crazy.

"Could you get me a blanket?" she says. "I'm just so cold. But for some reason, I don't have the energy to sit up."

I rush to get her a blanket, all the while thinking, *Why is she so cold? This makes no sense. It's still so hot outside!*

I put the blanket on her, gently tucking it around her.

Then I call Sam's mom.

Mrs. Samuels is a nurse. She's always worked the night shift—Sam told me she even did this when they lived in Chicago—so she can be home for her family when they're awake.

She comes right over, crouches on the ground beside Nana Anna.

"How do you feel?" she asks. "Is there any tingling sensation in your arms? Any numbness?"

"I don't know," Nana Anna says, her teeth chattering. "Maybe. I can't tell. I'm too busy shaking."

"I'm calling for an ambulance," says Mrs. Samuels.

I hold Nana Anna's hand until the ambulance

comes, telling her I love her, that she has to be okay. When the ambulance gets here, it is hard to let go of that hand, hard to watch them carry her away.

This all feels so wrong. How can Nana Anna be sick? She's the strongest person I know.

"Come on," Mrs. Samuels says after they leave. "I'll drive you to the hospital."

Walking into the hospital is so scary and unreal—*I shouldn't be here! I should be at home, laughing over dinner with Nana Anna!*—and yet there is something about walking into that sterile environment that somehow makes the unreal real.

This can't be happening to me, and yet it is.

"I want to see her," I tell Mrs. Samuels, feeling desperate. I will remain worried until I can *see* Nana Anna. That's the only way I'll know she's still alive.

"Later," she soothes. "They won't let you see her until after they've examined her. Here, while we're waiting, I'll help you fill out these forms."

Which she does.

Mrs. Samuels is a very cool customer—maybe working close to death every day has made her so—and she had the foresight to grab Nana Anna's purse before we left the house, so we will have all the information we need to fill out these endless forms.

We are there for hours, waiting, and during that time I start worrying that Nana Anna must have had a heart attack, suddenly remembering that time Margot came to dinner and Nana Anna had that episode.

Damn that Dutch food! Nana Anna has probably eaten herself into a coronary.

At last a nurse comes out and tells us we can see her now.

I don't want to see Nana Anna sick, I don't want to see her weak and in a hospital bed, maybe dying. Too many people have died on me already. But I do want to see Nana Anna. So I force myself to take the steps into her room.

It is so hard seeing her like this. She looks so small.

But at least she is awake. Alive.

I hold her hand, try to smile, listening as Mrs. Samuels talks to the doctor behind us.

"Is it her heart?" Mrs. Samuels asks the doctor in a hushed voice. "Lacey said something about her grandmother having an episode a few weeks back. Plus she takes heart medication."

"I'm afraid we don't know *what* it is at this point," the doctor says. "She hasn't had a heart attack, but we'd like to keep her here for observation and run some more tests."

I don't want Nana Anna to stay in the hospital. I want her to come home with me. But I also want her to be well again, and if staying here will make her that way . . .

"I'm sure they think I can't hear them," Nana Anna whispers to me with a tiny smile, "because I'm practically an old lady. But what they don't know is, this old lady can still hear twenty-twenty."

I laugh at her joke, relieved that she can make one.

"When you get home," Nana Anna says, turning serious, "call Aunt Helga." She's referring to her older sister, my great-aunt. "Have her come stay with you. You shouldn't be alone. You're too young to be alone. I've got great insurance, never use it—they'll probably keep me in here running tests forever."

"Just get better," I tell her, praying with all my might that this will happen. "Please, just get better."

.   .   .

After visiting hours are over, Mrs. Samuels drops me off at home. I thank her for all her help.

"Don't forget to call your aunt," she reminds me just before I close the car door.

Inside the house, still in obedient mode, I go immediately to the phone to call Aunt Helga. I'm halfway through dialing the number when I stop.

I picture what having Aunt Helga here, for however long it takes Nana Anna to get better, will be like.

Put it like this: Aunt Helga makes Nana Anna look modern. She wears lace-up boots with her polyester housedresses, and her hairstyle looks like something women wore a hundred years ago. Worse, much worse, she is a Chatty Cathy. All the woman does is talk-talk-talk and never about anything important. She'll tell you all about her neighbors' kids, what kind of deal the guy down the street got on his house, how the priest at her church performed a miracle during a counseling session by busting up some mismatched couple who were planning on getting married.

Every time she talks on the phone with Nana Anna, I hear Nana Anna saying, "Why do you tell me this stuff, Helga? I don't know these people. Why should I care?"

I think Aunt Helga must do it because she's lonely. But I can't have her here, filling up my head with all her empty chatter. Nana Anna getting sick is the biggest thing that's ever happened to me, and I just can't take the noise. I need to think.

Yes, I know I should tell Aunt Helga that her sister is sick. But if I do that, her Chatty Cathy-ism will only make Nana Anna feel sicker, so I resolve to call Aunt Helga only after we find out what's wrong with my grandmother and if it's serious.

But no sooner do I set down the phone than I notice how *wrong* the house feels right now. It's not just that there are no cooking smells in the air, it's that there's not the sound of Nana Anna, the mere huge presence of her, either. And suddenly I feel really lonely and I realize that ever since my parents died, Nana Anna has been the one constant buffer between me and loneliness.

This house is so empty without her.

I go to the sofa and pick up the blanket I wrapped her in earlier. I hold it to my nose, breathe in deep. This, at least, still has the scent of her.

Then I start to cry.

It's going to be a long night.

12.

THE NEXT DAY I PHONE THE SCHOOL AND
say I won't be in. Usually an adult has to call a
student in absent. But when I explain about Nana
Anna being in the hospital, the secretary is all
sympathy.

"How long do you think you'll be out?" she asks.

"I don't know," I say. "As long as it takes."

I tell her I'll keep up with my schoolwork. Margot
will bring my assignments home for me. We always
do that for each other when one of us is out sick.

I hang up, but my hand hovers over the phone.
I've been waiting for the perfect opportunity to call
Chad again, and in a way this is it: I have the house
to myself. But somehow I can't think of Chad right
now. All I can think of is Nana Anna as I lift the

phone again, using it to call a taxi to take me to the hospital.

Nana Anna doesn't seem any better. If anything, she seems—I don't want to use the word "worse"—weaker.

I hold her hand, try to get her to eat, but she's not interested in food. I try to engage her in the TV suspended in one corner of the room—Nana Anna loves soap operas, particularly the ones in Spanish, even though she doesn't speak Spanish—but even that holds no appeal.

So I just start talking, rambling about anything I can think of. I tell her about the other girls on the cheerleading squad. I tell her about the new kid Liam Schwartz and how Margot has a crush on him and calls him SchwartzDreamy. I even tell her about screwing up on my two English papers but how it's all somehow working out.

"I swear," she says, yawning, "you're talking so much, you're beginning to sound just like Helga. How is Helga, by the way?"

"She's fine," I say, which I don't *think* is a lie. True, I never called Aunt Helga to come stay with me, like

I was supposed to. But the woman is a battleship. I'm sure that wherever she is, she's fine. The Helgas of the world always are.

"Why didn't Helga come with you today?" asks Nana Anna.

"Excuse me?" I sit up straighter, aware that something is happening that I hadn't planned on.

"I said," Nana Anna repeats with more patience than she would if she weren't so sick, "why didn't Helga come with you today? I would think my only sister would be here."

"Oh, you know Aunt Helga," I say with a nervous laugh. "As soon as she arrived, all she wanted to do was give the place a good seasonal cleaning and rearrange the cabinets the way *she* thinks they should be organized."

"Helga." Nana Anna gives a halfhearted snort. "She's probably already whisked the dishwashing liquid from the right to the left side of the sink." She gives a mild *tsk* and a headshake. "Wrong, wrong, wrong."

"Exactly," I say vehemently. "You don't even want to *know* which way the toilet rolls are spinning now."

"Oh, God in heaven." Nana Anna groans. "Don't tell

me the toilet paper now comes down over the top?"

"I told you that you didn't want to know," I say. "So, you see, Aunt Helga is very busy being . . . Aunt Helga. I'm sure if there was really something to worry about, with you being in the hospital, she'd be right here. As a matter of fact, you could probably use it as a barometer of how sick you are: So long as you don't see Aunt Helga, it means you aren't getting any worse."

"She's not getting on your nerves, is she, with all her senseless chatter?"

"Oh, no. No, she's not bothering me at all," I say, which is totally true. How can I be bothered by her chatter, when she's not even there?

"That's good," Nana Anna says, yawning again. "I think I'll sleep for a little bit now."

And in a second, she's out.

"I love you," I say quietly, hoping she can hear me in her sleep.

Watching her sleep, a wave of guilt overtakes me. I'm relieved that Nana Anna believed me about the reason why Aunt Helga hasn't come to see her, but I feel so guilty for lying. Nana Anna trusts me so much, I guess because I've always been such a good and well-behaved and honest granddaughter, that it would never even occur to her to check up on me to see if I'm telling the truth. Maybe it's that she's so weak from being sick, she doesn't have the strength to call the house to see if Aunt Helga's there. But somehow I think that, even if she were feeling stronger, she wouldn't do it. She trusts me that much.

I give her one last kiss. Then I go in search of a doctor or a nurse, anyone who can tell me what is wrong with her, but nobody knows anything. They need to do more tests.

"Your grandmother will feel better if she knows you're taking care of yourself," one of the nurses advises. "It's probably more stressful if you're here every second. It'll make her feel like you're not enjoying your life."

How can having someone who loves you at your side be stressful? I wonder. But I take her hint and go home late in the afternoon.

"See you in the morning," the nurse says, knowing I'll be back.

When I arrive home to my empty house, there are two messages on the answering machine.

The first is from Margot.

"Omigod, Lacey, I'm so sorry! I can't believe Nana Anna is in the hospital! Please, call me as soon as you get in and let me know what's going on. Really, anything I can do to help, you know I'll do it."

I'd call her right now, but first I have to listen to the next message, which is from Kimmie.

"Bummer about that relative of yours. Anyway, the squad and I are all concerned. The next soccer game is Monday after school. Call me back and let me know if you'll be there, okay? We really need you."

I want to call Margot back first, but instead I call Kimmie, feeling as though I have to get her out of the way before I can get to Margot.

"Hang on," Kimmie says when she hears it's me. "Everyone's at my place. I'm going to put you on speakerphone."

"Hi!" says Sylvia.

"Hi!" says Heather.

"Hi!" says Missy.

"Hi!" says Amanda.

Even in the midst of crisis—mine and theirs— they're still the picture of perkiness. Well, if I could see them right now I'm sure they would be.

"For the record," I say, "'that relative of mine,' as

you put it, is my grandmother. She's my closest living relative."

"Oops, sorry," Kimmie says. "Even bigger bummer than I thought."

"And I don't know about Monday," I say, "but I doubt it. I'm going to stay home until Nana Anna comes home from the hospital." *If she comes home*, I can't help adding in my own mind.

"Nana Anna," Missy says. "That's a cute name."

"How unfair," says Heather. "You've only been a cheerleader for, like, a day, practically, and it's already all over for you."

"The pyramid will just be so lame." Amanda sighs. "It'll be like our point got shaved off the top."

"Yeah," Sylvia chimes in, "like Amanda says."

"Maybe Ms. Blackwell can get another eighth grader to take my place," I suggest.

"Are you kidding?" Kimmie says. "We already asked her. But when Ms. Blackwell told us about the qualifications of the other girls, we figured we'd pass. You're the only eighth grader we'd have."

There's something mildly satisfying in that.

"I promise when I get back," I say, "to try to, um, fulfill my cheerleading duties."

We all decide this is fair.

I get them off the phone and start to call Margot but then stop. Maybe I should call Chad instead? This is the perfect opportunity. *I have the house all to myself*— this has become like a mantra to me. But somehow, having him over here is a lot more intimidating than going to the movies with him. And it just feels so wrong right now. I mean, I still don't even know what's wrong with Nana Anna. And I just lied to her today about Aunt Helga. To have Chad over here so soon after lying about Aunt Helga would somehow feel like a double deceit. So, much as I'd like to see Chad, I call Margot instead. My relief is huge when I hear her voice on the phone.

"Can you come over?" I ask before even saying hello.

"I'm right there," Margot says.

Five minutes later Margot is at my door and then she's hugging me, crying.

It's my grandmother who's sick, and she's crying.

"I'm just so sorry," she says between sobs and hugs. "I'm sorry about all the fighting we've been doing. I'm sorry I wasn't here when you needed me."

"That's okay," I tell her. "How could you know this was going to happen?"

"I guess I couldn't." She sort of forgives herself, but then her resolve against herself hardens. "But somehow I should have known!"

I'm about to tell her again that it's okay when the phone rings.

It's Sam.

"I'm sorry," he says. "I know for as long as we've known each other I've always just stopped by without calling first, but when my mom told me what happened, I felt like it would be rude to just barge in. I don't know. You might want to be alone."

"I don't," I say. I can't believe how much better I feel, just hearing his voice. "In fact, Margot's here. Want to come over?"

After he says yes, I hang up the phone.

"Sam's coming?" Margot says, drying her eyes.

Margot and Sam used to see each other all the time around the neighborhood when he lived here before, but they haven't seen each other since he's been away.

"Yes," I say, "Sam's coming, and . . . omigod! I've got to go bind my breasts!"

"*What?*" Margot says, just one step behind me as I race up the stairs.

I rush into my room, find my gauze tape and Ace bandages.

"Lacey," she says, watching me, "I have no idea what you're doing, but I swear, that is gross."

"Never mind that now," I practically beg, "and please don't ask any questions." We both hear the bell. "Just go keep Sam busy while I finish up here. Please?"

I can tell she doesn't know whether to unlock the door or lock me away, but she does what I ask.

When I come down a few minutes later, bound breasts in place, Margot and Sam are in the middle of getting reacquainted. But then Margot looks at me, takes in my relatively breastless state, and shakes her head.

"This is just too weird," she mutters.

Sam seems puzzled by her comment but doesn't respond. And, just as I was struck moments ago by how much better it made me feel just to hear his voice on the phone, I'm struck now by how much better I feel seeing him.

"My mom said to ask about your great-aunt," he says instead. "She didn't see a car in your driveway."

"That's because I never called her," I admit.

"Omigod," Margot says. "You're here alone?"

"It's cool," Sam says to her. "I'll keep an eye on her." He says it with a new kind of confidence, like if he's keeping an eye on me nothing really bad can happen. He turns to me. "What should I tell my mom?"

I shrug. "That my great-aunt never learned to drive, she took the train here, and she hates the outdoors, which is why no one ever sees her outside?"

"Sounds good," Sam says. "Did you eat yet?"

I suddenly realize I'm starving.

"No," I say. "I haven't had anything since the Pop-Tart I had for breakfast."

"Why don't you cook something?" he suggests.

"Because I don't know how," I say without thinking.

"What about that cooking class you were taking?"

At the mention of "cooking class," Margot raises her eyebrows at me, but I give a slight shake of my head. This is not the moment to explain to her that I lied to Sam, telling him I was taking cooking and ceramics classes because I didn't want him to know I was cheerleading. I certainly can't tell her all that with him standing right there.

"Um, I guess I wasn't paying attention during the classes," I say lamely.

"No problem," he says. "I'll cook."

"*You* know how to cook?" I'm shocked.

"Of course." He shrugs. "With my mom's job, she can't be expected to do everything all the time." He must realize how adult his words sound, because he shrugs again, coloring slightly. "At least that's what she always says."

He goes to the kitchen, and Margot and I follow him.

He roots around in the cabinets and spice rack and fridge, lining up the ingredients.

"I can at least make a mean spaghetti with meat sauce," he says.

And that's what he does, showing me each step as he goes, so I can make it for myself.

He hands me an onion and tells me to cut it up into little chunks, but as soon as I slice into it I start to tear up. In a minute the tears come harder, and I don't know if I'm crying because of the onion or for fear about Nana Anna.

"Here," he says, gently taking the knife and the cutting board from me, "let me. I'll teach you how to cut up an onion without tears. Now, if we had time, I'd say to chill the onion for thirty minutes, because the sulfuric compounds within the onion don't react as strongly to the air when the onion's cold, but we're all pretty hungry here so I don't think we have thirty minutes."

"You sound like you're reciting something from a cookbook," I say. "What did you do, spend a year watching the Food Network?"

There's that blush again, coloring his cheeks. "Pretty much. When my mom told us she couldn't be expected to do everything around the house anymore, she gave me a cookbook and told me to go watch Rachael Ray. Anyhow, moving right along here . . . So we'll peel the onion, cut it in half, and let it soak in cold water for approximately ten minutes, like this. Then we'll light a couple of candles in the area where we'll be cutting the onion, like this, to draw the fumes away. Do you have a fan handy?"

I shake my head no, wiping at my eyes with the back of my sleeve.

"Too bad," Sam says. "We could have used it to blow the fumes the other way. But in the absence of that, we'll place the cutting board on the stovetop and turn on the exhaust fan. And we'll use distilled white vinegar to brush down the cutting board before slicing, like this. Oh, and it also helps if you can either keep your mouth closed or hold your breath while slicing."

I can't help it. I start to laugh. "This seems like an awful lot of steps to go through," I say, "just to save a few tears."

Sam's back is to me as he continues to work, so all I see is his shrug from behind when he says, "I just hate seeing you cry, Lacey. It's *wrong* somehow."

I don't know what to say to this. It's somehow such a serious thing for someone to say, particularly Sam, but before I can think of how to respond, he laughs and adds, "Oh, and don't forget to wash your hands with lemon juice after cutting up an onion. It cuts the smell, and there's nothing worse than making a terrific sauce, only to have your hands wind up smelling like onion all night."

I look at my friend, and it's kind of like I'm seeing him for the first time. It's shocking to realize there are things about him I don't know.

After dinner, I'm too tired to talk after a long day of worrying about Nana Anna, but my friends stick around, keeping me company as I watch TV.

It's good to have friends.

Margot goes to the bathroom, and I look over at Sam.

"You made dinner for me," I say, "and you're going to lie to your mom on my behalf. Why are you so good to me?"

"Because you're my best friend," he says simply.

When he says this I feel something . . .

I don't know. It's impossible to explain it.

Saturday and Sunday pass pretty much the same, with me making trips to the hospital and Sam or Margot or both keeping me company in between. Each day I think about calling Chad—like, a million times—but then reject the idea because it feels wrong somehow with Nana Anna still being so sick. Each day I try to tell myself Nana Anna looks like she's getting stronger. But who knows? Maybe I'm just lying to myself.

Then Monday comes and at last—at last!—the doctor has some good news for me.

"Your grandmother should be able to go home tomorrow," he says. "We've isolated the problem."

"What was wrong?" I want to know.

"A virus," he tells me.

"That's a code word," Nana Anna says, a mischievous look in her eyes for the first time since this started, "for 'they have no idea.'"

"Of course we know what it is," the doctor says, bristling, "and those antiviral drugs we've been giving you in that IV are solving that problem."

I don't care what it was. All I care about now is that whatever was wrong with Nana Anna is being taken care of, it wasn't a heart attack, and she'll be coming home tomorrow.

That's all I need to know.

And, in order to celebrate, when I get home I finally call Chad and invite him over. Now that Nana Anna is on the mend, I no longer have to feel *as* guilty about having a boy come visit me in the house when I know deep down that Nana Anna wouldn't approve of such a visit.

I invite him over to my house where there is, at present, no adult supervision.

13.

THIS CALLS FOR THE BIG GUNS.

I get out the crimson satin top, the one that shows off my cleavage, and put it on over a pair of jeans.

I forgo the makeup, previous experience having taught me I'm no good at it.

One of Nana Anna's many aprons covers my shirt as I cook, because I don't want to splatter red sauce all over myself. I'm making the spaghetti and meat sauce Sam taught me to make, the one dish I've mastered. I've turned on the CD player, and I hum along with the music as I stir the pot.

When the doorbell rings, I quickly lose the apron, giving my hair one last fluff.

Chad looks gorgeous standing there on my doorstep, and I can't believe he's brought flowers.

"Wow," he says, with a nervous laugh, "this house is really pink."

"You saw it before," I remind him as I go into the kitchen, figuring that if someone gives you flowers—no one's ever given me flowers before!—you're supposed to put them in a vase.

"Yeah," he says, "but, I don't know, I guess I forgot how pink it was."

Flowers taken care of, I turn to go back to stirring my pot and nearly bump into Chad.

Before I know it, his arms are around me and he's kissing me. It feels good, of course, but somehow it feels different than the times he's kissed me before. Before, it was either in the car and I knew I was going straight home or it was after the game when other people were standing around. But this—it feels like the second kiss that first night, only this time there's nowhere else for me to go.

Gently, because I don't want him to think I don't want to kiss him, even though I don't want to kiss him right *now*, I push him away.

"I'm sorry," he says. "I just couldn't wait to kiss you. I've been wanting to do that again for so long."

"Of course," I say. "I've wanted that too, but—"

"And that shirt, Lacey." He looks me up and down, a smile of appreciation on his face as his eyes flash wide. "You look so great in that shirt."

"Thanks," I say, blushing, "but I really need to stir the pot before things burn."

"That smells good," he says. "But you never said, how come you have the house to yourself tonight?"

"Because my grandmother's in the hospital," I explain, "but she's coming home tomorrow."

"Your *grandmother* is in the hospital?" He looks shocked. "And you never thought to call me?"

Why *didn't* I call him? I honestly don't know.

"I don't know," I say, trying on a casual tone of voice. "I guess everything just happened so fast."

"You could have called me," he says. "I could have been there for you."

Dinner goes well.

At least the food part does. I've set the table with the good china and silverware. I even lit candles. Not having had a guy over for dinner before, all I know is what I've seen on TV.

But the conversation? Yeah, it's a little flat.

The uncomfortable thought occurs to me: I don't

really know a whole lot about Chad Wilcox. I mean, I know that he's gorgeous, that he's old enough to drive, that he goes to a different school from me, and that he plays a mean game of pinball. But what else do I really know?

Oh, yeah, that's right: I also know he's a good kisser, which he reminds me of once again as soon as dinner is over.

He places his linen napkin by his plate, gets up from his chair, comes around the table, and crouches down beside my chair.

"That dinner was great, Lacey," he says, taking my hand. Then he kisses me.

It's a good kiss, a great kiss even, and it goes on and on as he helps me rise from my chair, walking me from the dining room to one of the sofas in the living room, kissing me all the while, sitting me down on the sofa, kissing me, kissing me . . .

Okay, it's a stupendous kiss.

This kiss . . . I could live inside this kiss forever.

He pulls away just long enough to observe, "Wow, there sure is a lot of furniture in this room," before going back to kissing me.

It's just what I need, these kisses, a release after

the past days of worrying about Nana Anna.

But then the kissing gets deeper, more probing, like the second kiss that time in his car, and I pull away from him.

"TV!" I say brightly. "Would you like to watch some TV?" I scramble for the remote, which I suddenly can't seem to figure out how to use. "I swear," I say, frantically pushing buttons, "there's this really great program on tonight. In fact, I'm pretty sure it's going to start right now!"

"I don't want to watch TV right now," he says, gently prying the remote from my grip and dropping it on the side table. "I want to do this, Lacey."

And then he kisses me some more and it's so good, I start living inside it again.

In fact, I'm so busy living inside this kiss, I barely notice it when Chad's hand moves from the small of my back, moving up over my shoulder to the front, inching its way down until it's at the top hook and eye of my blouse.

But I definitely feel it when all the hooks and eyes on my crimson blouse come apart.

"You're so beautiful, Lacey," he says, gazing down at my bra.

Whatever I may be ready for in life, I'm not ready for this.

I push away from him with one hand, while with the other I grab at the separated sides of my blouse, trying to hold it together.

"I'm *twelve*!" I blurt out.

"*What?*" His blurt is even louder than mine as he jumps backward away from me, sending himself over the end of the sofa. He scrambles to his feet and takes another step back. "But that's impossible!"

"Of course it's possible," I say, angry, doing up my hooks and eyes all the while. I know it's not fair to be angry with him. He didn't know I was only twelve. He didn't know because I never told him, but still. What I really am is angry with myself, and embarrassed that I was just stripped down to my bra for all the world to see, but it comes out as anger at him.

"But you said—"

"No, I didn't. You assumed." I start feeling a bit guilty. "And I never corrected your assumptions."

He starts backing toward the door, hands held in front of him defensively. If I weren't so upset about everything that's happened, everything that *is* happening, I'd be laughing. A few minutes ago he was pulling apart my shirt, and now he looks like he's scared that *I* might attack *him*!

"So that's it?" I call after him. "It's over?"

He stops backing up. "Well, yeah." He looks surprised, but then his expression softens. "I'm sorry if you're hurt, Lacey. But I can't go out with you anymore." And then his expression hardens again and I have a flash where suddenly I see him looking at me the way Mr. Fitzgerald looked after class that day I had my cheerleading uniform on. It's as though he has to keep a safe distance between us. "You're not even in your teens yet!"

I hate to admit it, but he has a point.

Still, I have to try.

"But we can start over again, right?" I say. "Look, I'm sorry I didn't tell you the truth right away. I know I should have. But that first day, when we met at the mall, it was so great." I smile, remembering that day, the simple ease of meeting a guy I had something in common with, without him making me feel all weird, like an object. "You obviously liked me, and I liked you, but I realized you thought I was older and that if you knew I was younger you'd never like me, not in that way. But now you have liked me for a long time—*me*—without even knowing how old I was. So maybe we could start again now that you do know, only this time we could take things slower and—"

Okay, I'm babbling here. And if I didn't know that already, I'd know it by the way Chad is slowly shaking his head.

His expression softens once more. He approaches me, puts the palm of his hand gently against my face.

"I'm sorry," he says. "You're a great girl, Lacey. Maybe when you're a few years older, but not now. You're twelve, Lacey. *Be* twelve."

Then he kisses me one last time, softly on the lips, and he's gone.

The door is barely shut when I start to cry. I don't even know why I'm crying, but it feels like I've lost something—not Chad, not that, but something big.

And so I cry.

I'm still crying when there's another knock at the door.

Maybe Chad has come back?

I wipe at my eyes, hoping.

But when I answer the door, it's not Chad. It's Sam.

"Hey," he says, "I didn't phone first because my mom called me from work with the good news: Nana Anna is coming home tomorrow!"

He must see the way I look, though, the tears staining my cheeks, because his expression of joy changes.

"Lacey, what's wrong?" He hooks his thumb over his shoulder, indicating the curb. "Hey, there was a car parked out there for a while. Now that I think about it, it was the same car that came by the day you and I played catch. Was that guy bothering you?"

I can't help it: I start to cry again.

I know I'm acting totally childish; a part of me knows what I had with Chad wasn't anything real anyway, not if it was based on lies and could evaporate so quickly, but I still cry.

Sam takes me in his arms, soothes me. In a dim part of my brain, it occurs to me that I'm not in my "hide-my-breasts-from-Sam" mode. On the contrary, I'm wearing that damn crimson top in which all my bodily attributes are on display. Sam must feel that, he must feel the real me against his body as I cry into his shoulder.

But my best friend doesn't pull away.

. . .

I tell Sam all about Chad.

It's not my finest hour, I'll grant you, owning up to all the stupid things I've done.

And Sam doesn't take it very well.

"Lacey, how could you be so *stupid*?"

I'm a little surprised at his reaction. It's more the sort of thing I'd expect from Margot.

His disapproval sets off a fresh spout of tears.

"Oh, now, don't *cry*," he says.

I go to wipe my tears with the sleeve of my blouse but he stops me.

"And don't do that, either," he says. "You'll ruin your pretty blouse. It does look pretty on you, by the way. Um, very."

So he has noticed.

Well, and how can he not? I'm all cleavage in this shirt, all Lacey Underwire. But he's probably just saying that part about looking pretty just to be nice.

"Wait here," he tells me, "and don't use that sleeve."

He disappears from the room, returning a moment later with a handful of Kleenex. Gently he dabs the tears from my cheeks, then holds a tissue to my nose, instructing me, "Blow."

Once I've obeyed—spectacularly loudly, I might add—he disappears again. I presume it's to discard the icky Kleenex. When he returns, his expression is stern and he returns to, "Lacey, how could you be so *stupid*?"

I'm tired of crying, so, choosing to argue instead, I open my mouth to object to this accusation of stupidity, but Sam cuts me off.

"Lacey, you could have been hurt, *really* hurt. Why did you let that guy go on believing you were older?"

"I wanted him to like me, and I could tell that he did. I thought if he knew the truth, he'd stop liking me."

"Exactly. I mean, of course he wouldn't totally stop liking you. You're very likable."

I am?

"But," Sam goes on, "he'd have stopped liking you *in that way*."

This is something I'd suspected all along, and it was the reason I'd deceived Chad. Of course he wouldn't have gone on liking me *in that way* if he'd known I was only twelve.

"I'm just so *angry* at you right now, Lacey. It's not just that this was a stupid thing to do. It was a reckless thing. What if you hadn't finally told him you were twelve? What would have happened? Or what if after you told him you were twelve, he didn't care? What if he tried doing other . . . *stuff*?" Sam pauses, almost looking scared as he asks, "He didn't try doing other stuff . . . did he?"

"God, no!" I shake my head vehemently. "All he ever did was kiss me!"

There's a look in Sam's eyes now, I'm not really quite sure what it is.

"Yeah," he says, "I can see why he'd want to do that." And then he quickly adds, "You know, with him thinking he was on a date with you and all."

"You've never been angry like this with me before," I say, "not even that time when I was six and I broke your plastic bat by accident."

He gives a lopsided grin. "Well, that was a little different from this."

Right now I feel so upset, even more upset than I was when Chad . . . put the moves on me. Sam's never been angry with me before. Margot has, many times, but never Sam. What will I have, who will I be, if I lose his friendship?

"Just because I'm angry with you doesn't mean I'll

stop being your friend," he says, as though reading my mind. "I just want you to promise me you'll never do something this stupid again."

I make that promise, relieved there's something I can do that'll make him smile at me again.

"Why can't you just go for guys who are your own age?" he asks.

I think about the guys in my class who, even though they're all one and two years older than me, are probably the kind of guys he has in mind. John Fredericks, Fred Johnson, Liam Schwartz.

"Because they're all dorks?" I say, trying on a smile.

"Yeah," he says, but he's not smiling back, "yeah, I guess that's it."

After a bit, Sam leaves and I make my way through the bottom half of the house, making sure the doors and windows are locked, the stove turned off, the lights out.

Up in my bedroom, I take off my jeans and the crimson satin blouse. I move to throw the blouse in the garbage basket by my desk—a fat lot of good that blouse did me!—but something stops my hand

and instead I put it in the laundry basket to be cleaned. I can't imagine ever wearing it again, and yet it feels as though I should keep it as a reminder of . . . something.

But I do throw away something else: the tape and Ace bandages I've been using to camouflage my breasts from Sam. After tonight, the cats are out of the bag, so to speak, and I won't be needing those anymore.

I do my getting-ready-for-bed routine and then climb between the sheets. Then I lie there, gazing up at the ceiling as the moonlight peeks in through the blinds, wondering about my talk with Sam. I wonder how I got to be the kind of person who could get herself in a situation like the one I was in with Chad tonight and wonder how I can find the road back to being the person I really am, or maybe even just discover who I am after all.

Tomorrow Nana Anna will be coming home.

14.

ON TUESDAY, MRS. SAMUELS DRIVES ME to the hospital to pick up Nana Anna and bring her home. Mrs. Samuels usually sleeps a lot when Sam's at school during the daytime, since she works the night shift, but she says this is too important a day for me to be picking up my grandmother in a cab.

I expect Nana Anna to look frail, as she has ever since she first got sick, but when we get to her room she's dressed and raring to go.

"Let me get at that house," she says to me with a twinkle in her eyes. "I'll bet you haven't even dusted since I've been gone."

Oops, I think, but I smile back.

Then she adds, "Of course, Helga's probably dusted my furniture down to the point where there's not even any furniture left. Speaking of which, why didn't Helga come with you to get me?"

My heart thuds and I tell one more lie. "She's not here," I state the obvious. "She's, um, home, cleaning." There will be time to set the record straight. I just want to enjoy this moment: taking Nana Anna home.

I'm so glad to see her looking well and strong again. Nana Anna is bigger than life.

But as soon as Mrs. Samuels drops us off, leaving after she concludes that Nana Anna is healthy enough to be left with just me, Nana Anna suddenly looks like someone let all the air out of her tires.

"Here," I say, taking her elbow, "why don't you sit on the sofa and I'll make you some tea?"

"Since when do you know how to make tea?"

"I've never made it before, but I'm thinking you boil some water, then maybe throw a tea bag in it?" I shrug.

I come back from the kitchen a few minutes later, carefully carrying a mug of steaming tea.

"See?" I say, settling it down on the table in front of her. "I've started thinking cooking's not so hard after all. In fact, I could probably take over the cooking around here while you're still recovering."

"Huh," she says, lifting the mug of tea and sniffing it. Then she tilts her head back, sniffing the air.

My own sniffing talents? I inherited them from Nana Anna.

"Tomatoes?" She sniffs again. "Beef?" She looks at me. "Spaghetti with meat sauce?"

I nod.

"Did Helga make spaghetti with meat sauce last night?"

And now the moment of truth is here at last.

"Not exactly," I say, twisting my fingers together and doing a little guilty squirm. "I did."

"I see," Nana Anna says. Then: "So Helga showed you how to make it? This is why you are suddenly all-fired confident in the kitchen—because Helga has been teaching you things?"

"No," I say, and I can't delay it any longer, "Sam taught me."

"Oh. Sam. So Helga was supervising while Sam was teaching you how to cook spaghetti and meat sauce in the kitchen?"

"No." More squirming. "She wasn't."

"I see. And where is Helga, by the way? Even though you and Mrs. Samuels came to pick me up,

I would have thought she would at least stay long enough to greet me."

"She's not here." Biggest squirm of all. "She was never here."

"Oh." Nana Anna looks surprised. "Oh."

"I never called her," I admit. Then I continue to talk in a big rush. "I'm sorry. I know I should have called her. I should never have disobeyed you. But you know how Aunt Helga talks all the time. I couldn't stand the idea of her being here constantly, just talking-talking-talking when all I wanted to do was think of you, or her going to the hospital and talking-talking-talking at you until she made you crazy when you were supposed to be concentrating on getting better. I guess I just figured I could always call her once we knew what was really wrong, but then I never got around to it. Anyway, Sam promised he'd keep an eye out for me."

"Ah. So Mrs. Samuels knew you were alone here?"

"No. Just Sam. And Margot. I made them promise not to tell their parents."

She considers this. Then she looks around the room, as though assessing it for damage. She's sitting right on the sofa I sat on with Chad, but of course she can't see that damage. It's not visible.

"Everything looks fine here," she remarks at last. "I suppose I should be mad at you, though."

"Yes," I say simply, "you should."

"And yet," she goes on, "somehow I'm not." She shrugs, closing her eyes as though she's resting them. "Everything worked out fine in the end, didn't it?"

Well, sort of.

"And maybe you're growing up," she adds. "Maybe it's time I trusted you more to take care of yourself. Besides, Helga *is* an annoying person. So." She yawns, eyes still closed, stretching her arms out. "When is dinner?"

"You mean I'm not in trouble?"

"Of course you're in trouble. Just because I'm not mad doesn't mean you're not in trouble." She opens one eye. "Grounded from everything except non-school-related activities until further notice, and fifty lashes with a wet noodle. Now, when is dinner?"

After dinner, Margot stops by with my homework assignments for tomorrow.

"It's really good to see you, Nana Anna," she says,

giving her a hug and a kiss. "And you look great. I'll bet that before you know it, you'll be up and around and making us that pea soup with the mouse cookies again. I'd really like that."

"So would I," says Nana Anna.

Then Margot and I go up to my room.

As soon as the door is closed, I tell her what happened the night before. As I'm talking, I keep expecting her to interrupt with outrage. She's been so mad at me on the topic of Chad, I'm sure she'll be even madder now. And yet I can't not tell her. She's my best girlfriend and I'm tired of the distance between us. Still, when I finish, I wait expectantly, anticipating that she's about to pounce.

"Are you okay?" she asks.

"Excuse me?"

"After everything that happened last night with Chad—him trying to do, um, *other things*; him leaving when he found out you were only twelve—are you okay with that?"

I stop to think. It's a question I haven't asked myself yet. *Am* I okay with all this?

"Yes," I tell her, realizing the truth of it as I speak the words. "Yes, I am."

Margot shrugs. "Then that's all that matters."

"Wait a second here. You're not going to yell at me? You're not going to lecture me about how this is the stupidest thing I've ever done in my life?"

"Well, I have to admit, it *was* stupid. But no, Lacey, I don't want to lecture you. I want to apologize."

"Apologize? For what?"

"For being such a lousy friend these last few weeks. I should have been there for you. I should have listened to you, supported you when you wanted to talk about Chad, instead of judging you all the time." She shrugs again. "I guess I was just jealous of you. I realize it's not your fault. You can't help how you look any more than I can help how I look, but I guess I've always been jealous of you."

There. She's said it.

"But that's no excuse," she goes on. "You're my best friend. If I'd been there for you, maybe you would have called me last night after what happened. Maybe I could have helped you then."

I don't tell her that Sam was here last night, that Sam helped me. But inside, I smile at the memory.

"You're helping me now," I tell her honestly, and give her a hug. "So tell me," I say, drawing back, wanting to change the subject, "how are things going with Liam? Any news?"

"Oh, who knows?" she replies. "Who cares? Maybe he really likes me. Maybe he doesn't." She shrugs. "Maybe someday I'll find out which."

"Hey," I say, searching in the top drawer of my desk until I find what I'm looking for, "do you still have your own pair of these?" I wave my Wayfarers in the air, the ones we bought that day at the mall, that first day of school that seems a lifetime ago now.

"Of course," she says.

"What do you say we wear them to school tomorrow?" I put mine on. "We'll be the coolest thing Wainscot's ever seen."

"You're on," she agrees.

I close the front door behind Margot, after she makes Nana Anna promise one last time that she will make the pea soup and mice again really soon. Leaning with my back against the door, I think how Sam and Margot both know what went on here last night and that there's one person I still need to tell. True, earlier in the day Nana Anna had said, "Everything worked out fine in the end, didn't it?" But guilt is driving me now—the guilt of lying to Nana Anna that first time I went out with Chad, telling her I was going to Margot's house; the guilt of having him over last night, without adult supervision—and I just can't keep it in any longer.

Thank God it wasn't a heart attack that put her in the hospital after all, because if it had been, I'd give her a second one now.

"Nana Anna, can I talk to you?"

"Uh-oh."

"What do you mean, uh-oh?"

"It's never good when anyone says those words. It almost always means, 'Your car needs a new muffler' or 'I'm about to break your heart.' But okay." She smiles. "Let's talk."

So I tell her everything: about the first lies—how that first time Chad called it wasn't a boy from science class, but rather an older guy I met at the mall; how I lied about meeting Margot when really I went to the movies with Chad; about having him over for dinner while she was in the hospital. I finish by telling her how after Chad discovered I lied to him about my age, he basically dumped me.

"Are you all right?" is the first thing she asks.

This is the second time this has happened to me today: I expect people to be mad at me and instead they keep asking me if I'm all right.

"I'm fine," I say, "but aren't you mad at me for lying to you?"

"Disappointed? Yes. Mad?" She considers. "No. I'm not saying it's the best thing you've ever done—far from it—but I'm not mad. I guess, if anything, I'm sad; sad you didn't feel you could tell me the truth while it was going on rather than after the fact."

"But if I told you before, you'd never have let me go out to the movies with him or have him over here when you weren't home."

"A sixteen-year-old boy? Do I look nuts?" She laughs. "Absolutely not. But I do remember, hard as it may be to believe, what it was like to be young. And foolish. We all make mistakes. I'm just glad yours didn't cost you more."

I can't believe how cool she's being about this.

"And you're really not mad at me?" I press.

"No," she says. "You're growing up. Maybe we both are. Besides, I've already grounded you once. But tell me," she adds, "what made you think a sixteen-year-old boy was an appropriate choice for you?"

"I don't know," I say, honestly not remembering how I started on that path. "I guess I'm just starting to get more interested in guys, but the guys in my class all seem too young, and Chad just seemed . . ."

"Older. It must be confusing for you, Lacey—the changes your body has gone through; how the world reacts to those changes. Sometimes you look more like a woman than a girl, and I suspect the rest of the world sees you that way too."

"Well, yeah. I mean, I've got these two"—I look down at my breasts, grin lopsidedly, roll my eyes—"*luxe problemen.*"

"Perhaps," she says, "but they don't have to be a problem, not if you don't let them. Tell me: After all that's happened, do you still like this Chad?"

"God, no," I say right away. "I mean, you should have seen how quickly he jumped away from me after finding out I was twelve."

She surprises me by laughing a soft laugh. "I can imagine."

And suddenly I'm laughing too. "It actually was pretty funny. He fell right over the back of the sofa."

Her expression darkens. "You two were together on the sofa?"

Oops. Wrong thing to say. But rather than lying this time, I simply fail to address that question. Besides, she knows Chad was here, she knows what happened. "He could have at least offered to stay friends," I say.

"Yes," she says softly, "he could have at least offered that."

"It's important to have friends," I point out.

"Yes. Yes, it is."

"Sam's my friend. Sam's always been my friend."

"Yes. Yes, he has."

"Sam's a lot of fun." I think about how much fun we have together, playing catch and video games, and just generally laughing at the same things in life, like Tom Cruise running. "But not only that, even when I do incredibly stupid things, Sam's always there for me. I mean, *always*." I think of how he taught me how to cut onions properly, just because he didn't want me to cry, and about how he said he'd keep an eye on me while Nana Anna was in the hospital, and how much he helped me after Chad dumped me. "Sam never turns his back on me."

"Sam Samuels is a paragon of young manhood."

"And he's kind of cute, don't you think?" I remember how good he looked that night in the movie theater, when I was studying his profile in the dark. "I mean, he was always cute, even when I was a baby and everything was all 'gah' and 'goo.' But since he's come back? I think he's gotten, um, *guy cute*."

"No girl would kick Sam Samuels out for not being guy cute because he is certainly all that. Frank Sinatra would even say Sam has real fly-me-to-the-moon qualities."

"And Sam's also . . . he's also . . . omigod! I just realized: I like Sam! And I like him *in that way*."

"Yes, I can see that. But isn't this rather abrupt?"

"Abrupt? God, no! I've liked Sam my whole life. I've known him longer than anyone except for you, I just never really saw before, maybe because he was right under my nose. . . . But there's no way he'd ever like me back like that." As quickly as I've realized what I want—Sam—just as quickly I realize I'll never have it. "I mean, Sam and I have always been just friends."

"Hmm . . ."

"Hmm, what?" I say. My eyes narrow suspiciously. "What does that 'hmm' mean?"

"Oh, nothing," she says with a mysterious smile. "Just hmm." Then: "So, what are you going to make us for dessert?"

15.

ON WEDNESDAY I RETURN TO SCHOOL.
It's still fairly warm out, so once again I wear my white
blouse with the long-sleeved navy sweater draped
over my shoulders. On the bus, John Fredericks and
Fred Johnson fail to comment. Maybe everyone is
finally getting used to me. Or maybe we really are all
finally growing up.

But they all comment when Margot and I slip
on our Wayfarers while hanging out in front of our
lockers, and the comments are all positive. Maybe
we'll start a new trend? Margot loves the idea: us as
trendsetters.

Or maybe their comments are all positive
because they see first what I see now: Kimmie
Parker, followed by Sylvia, Heather, Missy, and

Amanda making another grand entrance in the middle school and heading straight my way.

"Hey, Lacey," Kimmie calls, "cool sunglasses. Ms. Blackwell told us you were coming back today. How's your grandmother doing?"

"She's much better, thanks."

"Glad to hear it. So, do you think you'll be up for cheering with us tomorrow? We've got another game."

"Yeah," adds Sylvia, "it would be really great if you could."

I think about it. Nana Anna really is a lot better than she was. When I left this morning, she was talking about regrouting the kitchen sink and maybe repainting the outside of the house dark purple before it starts getting cold out. So she doesn't really need me around to hover every minute. And while she did ground me from non-school-related activities, cheerleading is a school-related activity. Plus I like cheering. I like getting to use my body for something fun.

"Sure," I answer, "why not?"

"Cool," Heather says.

"Totally," Missy puts in. "When we tried to do the pyramid without you on Monday the top was too . . . what's the word I'm looking for?"

"Flat," Amanda provides. "It was flat."

"Yeah," says Missy, "totally."

"Well," I say, "I'm glad I can be of service in, um, keeping your top from looking flat."

English class is over and everyone is filing out when Mr. Fitzgerald asks me to stay a minute. Margot handed in my late paper for me while I was out, and I figure he wants to talk to me about that.

And, for once in my life—since it feels like I've been wrong about so much else lately—I'm right about something.

"Nice job, Lacey," he says.

I look at the top of the first page. There's a large A on it.

I know it's geeky to admit it, but I love getting As. It's a part of who I am. And I did write an A paper. Still, I can't accept this.

"I can't accept this," I tell him.

"What are you talking about?"

I think about how, that time when I was wearing my cheerleading uniform, he told me he'd give me an A if the paper warranted it, even though it was late. I think of the way he looked at me that day. Who knows? Maybe I was wrong about what I thought I saw. Maybe he wasn't checking me out. Or maybe, if he was, it was unintentional and the break he gave me had nothing to do with that. Maybe it's my own fault for seeing breast shadows everywhere, for seeing the world through breast-colored glasses. Maybe a good part of my problems comes down as much to how I see myself as it does to how the world sees me, or how I think it sees me. Whatever the case . . .

"I don't want any special favors," I say, not wanting to take any chances. "Dock me a grade, like you're supposed to. Give me a B. I've earned it."

I don't look back to see his expression after I hand him the paper and walk out.

Thursday comes and with it me in my cheerleading uniform and the game after school.

I cheer my heart out. It's not so much that I care if our team beats the other team. I mean, does it really matter? But it feels good to be letting off some noise after all the tension of worrying about Nana Anna plus the stuff that happened with Chad.

So I cheer, loudly, and I put my body through the pleasurable paces of jumping and kicking and doing splits and back handsprings. Despite the fact that I don't love heights, I even enjoy my time at the top of the pyramid.

Then the game is over and we have won and the cheerleaders are all congratulating one another on a game well cheered. I'm gathering my things together, preparing for the ride home with Kimmie, when I feel a tap on my shoulder, causing me to turn.

"Nana Anna! What are you doing here?"

I can't believe I didn't notice her before. But then, when you're cheering, you get so wrapped up in what you're supposed to be doing and what's going on in the game, you don't really notice specific faces in the crowd, not unless you're looking for them, like that game when I was looking for Chad.

"I wanted to see you in action for myself," she says. "Is that all right?"

"Of course it's all right."

"Good," she says. "And I hope it's also all right then that I brought a friend."

She steps aside and there, right there, is Sam.

I can't help it. Without thinking about it, the smile that stretches across my face is huge.

"Hey," he tells me. "You were really great out there.

I'm glad you haven't let your gymnastic training go to waste."

"Thanks," I say, still smiling huge. "But I don't understand. What made you come? How did you know?"

"Nana Anna told me."

I glare at her, but she stops my glare by putting a finger to her lips. Then she mouths, *Just listen to Sam* before strolling casually away.

"I guess, like Nana Anna," Sam says, "I, um, wanted to see you in action for myself."

"Okay."

"So, listen." He shuffles his feet. I can't believe it: Sam—*my* Sam—is shuffling his feet? "I was wondering . . . do you think we could maybe go to the movies together sometime?"

That's it? "Of course," I say. "We always go to the movies together. I mean, except for when we go with other people."

"That's not how I meant."

Then what? And then it hits me. "You mean like on a *date*?"

Sam practically winces at the word. Well, you have to admit, it is a pretty stupid word, and I wince too as soon as I see Sam's face. But:

"Yeah," he says, "sort of. Only without using that word for it."

But then something else hits me and I get angry.

"It's because I look different now, isn't it?" I say. "It's because I'm Lacey Pom-Poms."

"*What?*"

I feel my face redden at the thought of having to explain. "That's what some of the other guys call me, when they're trying to be mean: Lacey Pom-Poms."

"God, no," Sam protests. "You think I like you differently now because of your"—I can see he can't bring himself to say the word *breasts*—"pom-poms?"

I just glare at him.

"Are you kidding me, Lacey?" he says. "I've liked you since you peed in my sandbox. I've liked you since you stole one of my toy soldiers and gave him hair extensions. Do you really think I'm going to like you more now *just* because of your . . . pom-poms? I shouldn't have to point this out, but of all the people in this world, you can bet I like you for who you *are*."

Even someone who has lately been as frequently off the mark as I have can't miss the truth here:

Sam likes me. He even likes me *in that way*.

I wonder what it will be like going on a first

something-like-a-date-but-not-called-a-date with my best friend. Of course, either Nana Anna or Mrs. Samuels will have to drop us off there, which will be a little different than if we were able to drive ourselves, but that day will come. Still, I wonder what it will be like. I think it will be comfortable, because I know Sam so well, but exciting, too, *extremely* exciting, because our relationship is changing. *We* are changing.

"I like you for who you are too, Sam," I finally say, smiling, "and my answer to your question is yes."

16.

TORPEDOES.

Bazooms.

Balloons.

Knockers.

Boobs.

As I prepare for my first something-like-a-date-but-not-called-a-date with my best friend—by the way, two things I am *not* going to be wearing are the crimson satin blouse *or* the SPANKY'S FRANKS T-shirt—I think of all the things people have said to me about my breasts and how those people have looked at me. And I see something now that I didn't see before: It was never just about other people reacting to me, it was also me reacting to their reactions and me simply reacting to myself.

But I'm more than just my breasts; I see that now. Actually, I'm much more, and they're really just a tiny percentage of my body and something over which, as Margot pointed out, I have no control.

I'm not my breasts. I never have been.

I'm just Lacey Underhill, and that's fine.